Jane in St. Pete

by

Cynthia Harrison

A Jane in St. Pete Mystery, Book 1

Jane in St. Pete

Cover Art by *Diana Carlile*

The Wild Rose Press, Inc.
PO Box 708
Adams Basin, NY 14410-0708
Visit us at www.thewildrosepress.com

Publishing History
First Crimson Rose Edition, 2020
Trade Paperback ISBN 978-1-5092-3335-9
Digital ISBN 978-1-5092-3336-6

A Jane in St. Pete Mystery, Book 1
Published in the United States of America

Her doorbell rang, much louder than usual. She needed coffee and aspirin. But she dutifully went down the hall and peered into the tiny video camera at the front door.

George, her neighbor. She didn't know him well—he'd just moved in—but he was also from Detroit, so, despite his youth, which kicked her out of her position as youngest owner in Winding Bayou, she let him in. George didn't bat an eye at her cut-off jean shorts, baggy sleep shirt, or bed hair. Jane had to stop herself from trying to smooth down her rioting curls. She folded her arms across her shirt because she wasn't wearing a bra. He didn't notice. His eyes were wild with panic.

"What is it?" Jane motioned for him to come in and follow her down the hall. "Sorry. Late night. I need coffee."

She poured two cups and nodded to George to take one before she grabbed the aspirin bottle from the cupboard. She threw some pills down her throat and slurped a long sip of coffee. She was still waiting for George to speak. He had tried to lift his mug of coffee, but his hands trembled so violently that the coffee sloshed onto the countertop. She'd drained half her cup by this time, so she set it down and repeated her first words to him. "What the hell is wrong, George?"

He fell into a seat at the snack bar separating her galley kitchen from the sunroom. He gouged his eyes with the heels of his hands. "I don't know where to start," he moaned. "Okay. So. There is a very bloody shirt—it's dried blood—on the front seat of my car. There are a ton of cops outside the gate. Have you not heard the sirens?"

Praise for Cynthia Harrison and...

LILY WHITE IN DETROIT:

"An entertaining mystery with more than just a hint of romance…an intriguing and enjoyable read."

~

"I warm to emotionally damaged loners in novels. I liked the picture of Detroit in the 21st century."

~

"All the characters are well written, but I especially liked the two main characters, such lovely chemistry."

Dedication

This is for all my fabulous Florida friends.
Sorry I moved some of our favorite places around. For plot purposes, I had to play with names and geography in our beloved St. Pete.

Chapter One

Jane Chasen stood just inside the doorway of the Winding Bayou clubhouse. Animated noise bounced off the walls as everyone talked and laughed. This coffee social happened once a week, but it had taken Jane months to finally walk down from her condo. She scanned the suntanned faces for Kim, one of the few people she'd met since moving here in the heat of July. Jane's husband had died in June.

Her hesitation in the doorway wasn't because she didn't want to make new friends. She simply had not found her social footing. Despite her silvering hair and the coral and pink outfit blending so well with the other soft pastel people, she didn't fit here yet. And not because her skin was so pale. Her mom had been right. She'd moved too fast. After Stan died, she'd rushed from a familiar world into the new. In a whirlwind blur, she'd buried her husband, seized early retirement, sold the house in Detroit, bought a condo in St. Pete, and left friends she'd loved forever. She consoled herself. Many of her friends would snowbird south come winter. They had rentals down the gulf coast from Sarasota to Naples.

But they weren't here now. Not in November.

Where was Kim? Jane couldn't stand at the door forever like a shy teenager at a dance. She headed for the coffee urns across the room. Round tables flanked both sides of a raised stage where a white-haired woman, clothed in soft coral, reigned at a grand piano, tinkling out a tune Jane could not hear over the caffeinated conversations. Jane was used to sizing up a room and estimating how many people filled the seats, used to marching to the podium and standing in front of a room full of strangers. This was not that. Her career was over. She'd be giving no art lecture today. But she did have an art-related question she needed to ask Kim and as many other people as she could meet. Why had it taken her so long to make nice with the neighbors?

Her former life erased itself as she deliberately built a new one. First, she'd had to buy furniture and clothes and silverware and, well, everything. She hadn't kept anything from her long marriage to Stan except photos of their children and legal paperwork. Now, phase two. Find some friends. She was here to drink coffee with a hundred people in a room that could sit three times that. Linen-covered tables ran the length of the dance floor, displaying a vast array of doughnuts glistening under the disco ball. Kim had mentioned they held dances here every weekend, with live bands. Jane loved dancing. Determined to fit in, she had donated her coffee dollar and bought a ticket to Saturday night's dance.

Since she'd arrived in St. Pete, she'd had a burning question she hoped someone here could answer. She clung to the idea of Waylon Silvercloud's amazing yard like a life raft as she made her way to the coffee line. She might not be lecturing on art anymore, but she still knew art when she saw it. And she wanted to get to know this man and his art better.

The scene began to settle as more coffee people

grabbed doughnuts and took seats. Jane stepped with feigned confidence toward one of the two large coffee urns. Styrofoam cups! She and her styrophobia had been prepared for this. She filled her own beautiful ceramic mug, something she'd found at the Dali Museum downtown. She added cream as she spied an empty chair close by. The people at the table included her new neighbor Kim, who waved Jane over. Good.

"Saved you a seat," Kim said, patting the chair next to her.

"Thanks, Kim." Jane smiled at the small group of people Kim was now introducing. There were more women than men, which was the general trend in Florida so no surprise.

Winding Bayou was a fifty-plus community, and from what Jane could see, at fifty-five, she might be the youngest person in the room. A welcome change from her lectures, which were usually held on college campuses or in art museums. The college kids came, not to hear her, but because their professors made it an assignment. There'd been a lot of ripped denim and bored faces. The museum attendees were more attentive, but their wardrobe color of choice was predominantly black. And nobody in Detroit, even friends older than her, had natural hair. Every woman she knew back home was ten shades of shiny gold-blonde.

And some of them had been less than kind when Jane's sensitive scalp had forced her to let the gray grow out. One acquaintance said she'd aged ten years overnight. Another had said "for lack of a better word" the color was "dull." Jane didn't know how to respond to people who said things like that out loud. But what she thought inside her own mind every time the mirror disappointed her with a new wrinkle or another jowl, was that those were signs she was supposed to focus on the inner work of life now, the work of preparing for what was to come. Stan's death had shown her how swiftly life ends. Death was a snap of the fingers.

Meanwhile, she still had some living to do.

"Widow or divorced?" asked the man sitting on Kim's other side. What was his name? Rich Something. His rude question didn't require a polite response. Jane turned to Kim, her eyebrows raised.

"Don't mind him," Kim said. Then she elbowed Rich and said, "Widow. She lives just above me. Be nice to her." Kim shook a finger at Rich, who pretended to bite it.

Conversation bubbled around her about people and places she didn't know. It felt like turning on a movie an hour into the story. She sipped her coffee and studied the people at her table. There were three other widows, making five with her and Kim. Then the one hopeless guy, Rich, and two married couples. Kim had introduced her to everyone, but putting names to faces eluded Jane.

She waited for a lull in the conversation so she could bring up Waylon Silvercloud. Silvercloud lived on Orange Blossom Avenue, in the block of old cracker houses shaded by trees hundreds of years old, just outside the newer, gated community. She wondered if others had observed what she had about his property. She threw the question out there. "Anybody else notice that yard of Waylon Silvercloud's?"

"You mean the Indian? With the totem poles in his yard?" asked one of the married men with a faint grimace.

"It's a mess," the wife added.

Jane rested her attention on the opinionated couple. The husband had a rounded belly and was brown as a coconut shell. His wife had shiny platinum hair piled high on her head. Shame she and her husband didn't know a thing about art.

Jane had been visiting the St. Pete area every winter for twenty years. Her job had allowed her to make her own schedule, and she'd made sure to take two or three weeks of the wickedest Detroit weather to visit her parents here in St. Pete. When the kids were small, she brought them with her during school's spring break. Jane and her mother had hit every art gallery and museum downtown. There was the Dali, of course, and the Chihuly, and many more. Jane loved art, she always had, but she was not an artist. So she taught. And now her purpose here would be to look. To see. To learn.

"Brings down the housing prices for his neighbors, including us."

Jane jolted out of her own thoughts to listen to the other married guy, who had a broad New York accent. Everyone here in Florida came from somewhere else.

"Why do you ask, Jane?" This from Queenie, another of the widows, whose name struggled up from Jane's aging neocortex.

Jane smiled at her and made quick eye contact around the table. Everyone was waiting for her answer. "I think he's an artist. An outsider artist. I didn't see any totem poles, but when the sun shines on his yard, the entire space is like some dazzling alternate world. It's an installation."

Jane tried not to use art-jargon that might not be

understood, but she sensed that with this crowd, attention could only be held so long. Sure enough, a side conversation or two started up the minute she stopped talking. She heard a dismissive "hrmph" from Rich, but the others had moved on to new topics, passing a phone around and laughing about someone named Big Snapper, who liked to hang out near the pool.

"Jane," Hazel, the widow next to her, said, "do you use the pool?"

"No." Jane smiled at Hazel, realizing she knew another name.

Hazel leaned into Jane with the phone video of a seven or eight-foot long alligator sunning itself on the lawn between the bayou and the pool.

"There's no fence!" Jane said, alarmed.

"He doesn't come up to the pool area. Not even when grandkids are swimming." Kim patted Jane's hand. Jane made a note that when they visited, she'd drive her own grandchildren to St. Pete beach instead.

"What makes you say Waylon is an artist?" Kim asked.

Hazel put her phone away and turned to talk to Queenie about the reading group meeting later today in the library. The married couples discussed dinner plans. Rich leaned in across Kim to hear Jane's response. Kim slapped his shoulder.

"Ouch," Rich said, not moving or taking his eyes off Jane.

"Well, it's just a sense I get driving past his home. It's difficult to be specific, but maybe the glass beading hanging from the palm leaves of his trees. Or the glint of copper objects planted in the side yard, poking out from the sawgrass. Reminds me of the Everglades."

Kim looked interested; Rich scowled, determined to find something to argue.

Jane threw him a bone. "You know the Seminole are the only unconquered tribe in America?"

"What? That can't be true. They've got a reservation, and that casino, right in Tampa!" Rich took the bait and chewed it.

"During the hundred-year war, here in Florida, the Seminole Nation hid in the Everglades and evaded capture. The copper pieces amid the tall grass reminded me of that historical fact." She'd found the information on Wikipedia, although she didn't know for sure if Silvercloud was Seminole or if his work represented his Native history. "I'm going to walk down there today to get a closer look."

"I'll go with you," Kim said.

"Not without me," Rich said.

Queenie leaned into Jane and whispered that she gave painting classes every Tuesday. "There're a dozen or so of us. The board even puts on an art show every year. You'd be very welcome to join."

Jane thanked Queenie, but she didn't feel the big *yes* inside that would signal her to go for it. Jane had never painted or sculpted, but she'd drawn in a notebook, with a pencil, most of her life. These days she preferred to look at art rather than to make it.

Kim and Jane left the auditorium the minute Rich got up to grab another doughnut.

"He's a bit much," Kim said, once they were clear of the building and walking the path to the gates. A guard on duty saluted them, and Kim smiled and waved.

"Rich got a crush on you?" This seemed obvious to Jane, but Kim denied it.

"If he has, he's got a funny way of showing it."

They strolled the four or five homes before Waylon's, all meticulously manicured with cypress and palm trees and clipped ornamental grasses.

"How many years have you been a widow, dear?" Kim asked.

"Not quite six months." The reason she'd sold the Detroit house was because Stan had died there. In the basement. Trying to fix faulty wiring.

"I'm so sorry. It will get easier." Kim squeezed Jane's arm. "It's been five years for me, and I still miss my husband every day. But I don't cry at night anymore. I have happy times and good memories. You will too."

Jane nodded. For her, life was already easier. Good memories? Not many of those. Fact was, she didn't miss Stan. For too many years, they'd had a marriage in name only. An effect of his workaholism meant he lost touch with his emotional side. Next, intimacy disappeared, according to Jane's mom, a retired psychologist.

Family birthdays, Christmas holidays, graduation parties, weddings, a baby grandchild—none of the milestones had been celebrations for Stan, only line items on a budget report. The kids, after college, both moved away for work, and Jane almost left Stan, but then her granddaughter came, so she'd postponed the divorce. The divorce lawyer said he'd keep her paperwork for when she was ready to file, which turned out to be never. The financial consultant she'd seen about dividing up all she and Stan had acquired during their marriage had ended up being a godsend when Stan died so unexpectedly. She told herself she would have gone through with the divorce, wished she'd done it years ago, but hindsight did no good, as her mother liked to remind her.

Kim gave Jane a quick hug, and Jane realized she'd sighed. Kim misunderstood, but this wasn't the time to set her straight. They'd arrived at their destination. Waylon Silvercloud's name was painted, first and last, in large block letters on his mailbox.

Jane took it all in. The mailbox, the road, the gate, and beyond. What appeared at first glance to be just another fence began to twist slightly out of your average white picket. As her gaze, and she supposed, the eyes of her neighbors too, moved beyond the dramatically ornamented fence, she saw, and all who looked would see, either the outsider installation or the motorcycle mechanic swigging beer in a yard full of junk and overgrown sawgrass. The perspective, she figured, depended on who was looking. Maybe only a person with an art background could see beyond the Harley under the carport, past the rusted lawn chair and the motor-oil-streaked fridge.

Today, Waylon wasn't out tinkering with his Harley yet, so Jane and Kim lingered by the fence while Jane tried to show Kim the artist, not the mechanic, without pointing fingers or being obvious. She started with the mosaic fence posts; bottle caps and beach glass embedded in concrete had a raw kind of beauty.

"See the way he's wound iron through the cement posts? The posts were certainly hand-poured. And he's got these found objects." Jane touched a polished stone. "He's even used refrigerator magnets."

"These are vicious points in the iron," Kim said, carefully touching a sharp tip of the unconventional fence.

"The iron looks hand-wrought," Jane said. "And when the sun hits it just so, like now, you can see the points are dipped in resin or gilt for a rainbow effect that kind of shimmers off the black."

Kim was silent, but she nodded as she tilted her head one way and then the other. Encouraged, Jane went on. "Look at the thick strands of beads wound around the bark and hanging with the palm leaves. I'm betting he hasn't fastened them in any harmful way. No nails on the tree trunks or glue on the leaves. I wonder how he keeps the palmetto bugs away?" Jane was awed now that she saw it all up close. The guy was genuine, she was convinced.

Kim started to ask a question when Waylon came outside. He did a double take when he saw them really looking. He came at them with a heavy tool in hand but dropped it immediately when Kim cringed. Jane felt Kim's body relax as he continued toward them with a smile on his face and no heavy tool in his fist.

"So what do you think?" he called out.

It seemed to Jane that his eyes almost immediately dismissed her, like he understood in a glance that she had plenty to say, plenty of compliments to pay. Instead he looked to Kim, for her impartial opinion. Or maybe, like Rich, he was drawn to Kim's delicate beauty.

"I don't quite know what to think," Kim said. They stared at each other, then Kim looked past him to the carport area and its refrigerator full of beer, an ancient boom box, and of course the cherry red Harley. "Why don't you put the fridge magnets on your actual fridge?" she finally said.

He laughed then, and so did Kim. Why indeed, their laughter said.

Jane's peripheral vision caught someone approaching. A third woman opened the gate and strolled up next to Waylon. She didn't look at Jane and Kim. She had a lunch sack in her hand, and Waylon turned his weathered face toward her.

"Mary, meet Kim and…" His voice wandered to a stop. Jane helped him out.

"Jane," she said, thinking Mary must live on the block. She hadn't heard any car engine cutting off.

Mary smiled at Jane and Kim, then handed the sack to Waylon who stuck his nose in it and sniffed. "Ahhhh. Meatloaf. Thank you, sister." The two presumed-Seminole seemed to forget about the people on the other side of the fence. Jane stepped away, and Kim followed.

"Come back sometime, Kim," Waylon said. "I'll show you my etchings!"

Under her deep tan, Kim blushed.

****

Back behind their gated wall, Jane and Kim walked past the pool, past the bayou glistening in the sun just beyond. They stopped at the mailboxes, inserted keys, and gathered mail and parcels. Jane was a dedicated online shopper, so mail delivery was a highlight in her days. Jane was asking Kim what to wear to the Saturday night dance when Fred, the handyman, interrupted their chat with a sharp turn and abrupt brake of his golf cart.

"Hey, Kim!" Fred said, hopping out of his cart. "Any packages you need me to carry?"

"I'm not a delicate flower, Fred!" Kim said. "But no," she added.

Kim did seem like a delicate flower to Jane. She was tiny, slim, and stunning with her blue eyes and platinum curls. By the way she spoke to the men, Kim proved she had sturdy roots and a muscular stem.

Fred started in on a story about the cable guy. "He said he wasn't gonna fix our cable because it ran under the building."

Their condo had four stories. Cable had apparently been laid before building began, a few years ago now.

"Said he was just going to run a new cable and let the old one rot in the water under here." Fred nodded toward their building, toward the lush red- and pink-flowering hibiscus and vibrant green palms. Despite the season, heat shimmered in waves off the flora.

"What water?" Jane asked, looking past the pretty façade to the base of the building's structure.

Fred and Kim exchanged a pointed look.

"You know this here was built on a swamp?" Fred said.

"I've heard that," Kim said.

"No." Jane had not known. She bought this place off *Zillow* because the pictures looked so nice. And the real thing had lived up to the photos. Until now. When Jane was young, people in Detroit would joke about selling you swampland in Florida, but Jane hadn't thought such a practice would be legal. Once again she worried she'd been in too big a hurry to leave her complicated past behind. The police had tried to make something out of that, they'd even found out she'd seen a divorce lawyer, but as she was lecturing out of town at the time of Stan's death, she had an iron-clad alibi.

Clearly Stan had done himself in because he'd been too frugal to call an electrician.

Kim laughed and so did Fred.

"Say it ain't so!" Jane flicked away the painful thoughts of her too-recent past.

"Oh, he's serious," Kim said as Fred hopped back on his golf cart, executed a jerky reverse and sped away. "They filled in all this area way back before we were born."

"So, that giant sinkhole called the Sunken Gardens, that's what happens sometimes after you fill in swamp?"

"I guess. Sure is pretty though." Kim was right. For a sinkhole, Sunken Gardens was gorgeous. Nurtured back to its natural state, all manner of tropical plant and bird life flourished there for a tourist's delight.

"Let's get each other's info," Kim said, holding out her phone to Jane. Jane surrendered her own device, still thinking about living on top of a swamp. They traded phone numbers, and Jane put her phone in the pocket of her shorts. She had an awkward package requiring two hands to carry upstairs. Fred must have seen it sitting at her feet, but he hadn't offered to take it up for her.

"There's a widow's table at the dance. Sit with us Saturday," Kim said.

Jane loved music. Her parents had the radio on all the time while she grew up. Her dad played guitar and loved singing old folk songs. Jane grew up on classic rock, and then she predictably rebelled with punk. She hadn't done much dancing in Detroit after career and family arrived. Now her family was scattered; the kids had moved where the jobs took them, building careers and their own lives and families. Time for Jane to do as she pleased. Music was one wonderful thing about Florida. It played everywhere, and people her age danced every day from noon until night. Her dad had a semiregular gig playing his beloved folk music for an hour every other Saturday night at a fancy restaurant overlooking the Gulf. Jane and her mom never missed a show.

She let herself into the condo and didn't even open the package from Amazon before asking Alexa to play "Because the Night" by Patti Smith. Alexa obeyed. Jane kicked off her flip flops and danced barefoot in her living room.

****

Just before dinner, which was a bowl of her favorite coconut granola, Jane's phone rang. Marisol wanted FaceTime. It would be two p.m. in Seattle. The baby usually took a long nap in the afternoon. Little Suzy was almost two and not a baby anymore, as Marisol had pointed out repeatedly. Jane answered the phone, keeping that in mind. Also, Marisol did not like "Suzy" and strongly suggested Jane call her granddaughter Susan.

"How are you?" Jane said. Marisol's eyes were puffy, and her hair hung limp around her face. Jane wanted to brush it and put it up in a ponytail. She'd done that often when Marisol was young. Perhaps never pulling her own hair back was Marisol's small rebellion. Jane didn't see or hear the baby.

"Susan taking a nap?"

"Yeah. Listen. I don't know when she's going to wake up, and I need to say this."

Marisol blotted her reddened nose with a tissue.

Oh, boy. Jane wondered what was wrong now. Because with Marisol, it was always something. Jane's daughter was sensitive. But then, Jane had to admit, she'd come by it honestly. Jane had sensitivity to Styrofoam, and her startle reflex was off the charts. She wanted to ask Marisol if anything was wrong, how she could help, but Marisol had said "listen," so Jane did.

"You're glad he's dead, aren't you?" Marisol said. "Danny thinks so, too!" Then she blew her nose in defiance.

Jane's spirits sank faster than a sunset on the horizon. Marisol was talking about Stan. Her beloved father. The man Jane had not liked even a little bit by the time he died. But she wasn't happy that he'd died. Sure, it had saved her the time and money a divorce would have cost. Still. He was Marisol's father. Suzy's grandpa. Not that he'd ever met Suzy. Jane had gone out to Seattle on her own when the baby was born, then when she'd had her first birthday and again just a few months ago. Stan had never made time to fly out to Seattle. And it was too late now.

"No," Jane finally said. "I'm not at all happy about your father's death. It was tragic. He was too young to die."

"But you don't miss him."

Jane wouldn't lie to her daughter. She never had. She'd been polite to Stan, made family dinner, and set a place for him every night even though most often he came home long after the rest of them had eaten. She did his laundry. He prepared his own breakfast and packed his own lunch, but Jane had kept the cupboard and fridge stocked with his favorite foods. His special blend coffee and his organic chicken breasts.

"Well?" Marisol said.

Jane sighed. "I've been keeping myself too busy to think about your dad." Jane remembered when her children were small and she'd been a stay-at-home mom. She loved her babies, but endless days full of sameness stretched into sleepless nights, when one or the other of her kids would wake up for a feeding, a drink of water, or afraid of the monster under the bed. Then, there had been the time Danny was burning up with a fever and had to be admitted to the hospital. Jane had had to wake the neighbors at two a.m. to come stay with Marisol because Stan was at work. Doing a double shift.

She still remembered the sleepy pity in her neighbor's eyes when Jane had said Stan was working late. Maybe they thought he was having an affair. Maybe he was. Jane never knew for sure. He hadn't been having sex with her in those days. That's when the estrangement between them had begun, after Danny was born. Jane had been so lonely for adult company, she'd pounce on him the minute he came in the door. He'd told her to stop following him around like a damn puppy and give him a minute to unwind. She cried that day, telling her husband that Marisol had refused to take a nap and Danny was miserable with teething.

Stan told her to get over herself. Women had been raising babies since the beginning of time, he said. He was sick of working all hours to support everyone and then come home to a wife who looked like she hadn't showered or slept. Sometimes, that was true. It was harder with two than it had been with just Marisol. She'd finally broken down and called her mother for advice. Mom had her own practice, but she made time and started dropping in a few days a week after work. She'd kept coming until Marisol started school. Then her folks retired and moved to Florida.

Just as Jane had now done.

"Are you happy?" Marisol asked.

Jane knew this was a trick question. If she said yes, it would prove Marisol's point. If she said no, she'd be lying. Except, right in this moment, she was not happy. Her daughter was angry and exhausted. Jane remembered what that felt like.

"Honey, of course I'm not happy your dad's gone. I know how much you loved him. And he loved you." Jane wasn't sure Stan had really ever loved anyone except himself, but she wouldn't say that to her daughter. "I hate seeing you so sad." That was the truth, anyway. Jane had fooled herself, told herself that the kids didn't notice the distance between her and Stan. She'd kept up the façade, slept in the same room, even the same bed. It was a California king, and he slept gripping the very edge of the mattress, as far from her as possible, but the kids didn't know that. And most of the time, Stan had simply not been there. Not on weekends, not for weeknights, not for dinner or homework or parent-teacher conferences or...

"That's bullshit. You're a liar."

Suzy was crying in the background as Marisol disconnected without saying goodbye.

Chapter Two

The next morning, Jane called her mom. "Want to have lunch at that new place out your way?" She knew it was one of Dad's golf days.

"Sure. I could use some new clothes for the cruise, if you want to shop after."

Jane had forgotten her parents were going on a Mediterranean cruise. Three weeks, land and sea. They'd visit Athens and even the little island of Delos that was uninhabited but had once been the vacation island of Cleopatra. Her mom was determined to climb the steps up to some ancient goddess temple ruins. Jane had seen pictures, and there were a lot of steps. But her parents had kept active, and even well into their seventies, they ran circles around her.

"Sure. Sounds fun." They figured out a time to meet, and Jane showered and washed her hair. It was long enough now to pull it back off her face, and she used a product that tamed the Florida frizz. Her hair had completely changed since she'd gone natural. If she didn't blow it dry and use a flat iron immediately, her gray, silver, and platinum strands would curl into tiny tight spirals. Sometimes she left it like that. Today, she tamed it into a sedate clip at the back of her neck. And she put on a little bit of makeup, too.

Mom was already at the restaurant when Jane got there.

"Should we have a glass of wine?" Mom asked. "I always shop better after wine."

"Yes, sure," Jane said. She could use it after Marisol's call last night. It felt like she'd been dodging emotional bullets her entire life, and now one had hit her. She was bleeding out. And her astute mother saw it right away.

They had a sip of wine as Jane wondered how to, or if she even should, bring up Marisol's harsh words. Jane was so close to her mother, and she'd hoped for the same kind of relationship with Marisol. That hadn't happened. Now Jane knew why. Marisol must have always sensed the problem in her parents' marriage. And she blamed Jane.

"What is it, honey?" Mom said.

Jane took another sip of wine and set the glass down. The server approached them, asking how they liked the wine and if they were ready to order yet. They both got salads, and Jane waited until the server had finished fussing with refilling their water and asking if they wouldn't like soup with their salad. Soup, when the temperature was a sweet eighty-five degrees. No thanks.

"Maybe dessert later?"

The server finally left to fill their order after Mom replied, "Maybe."

Jane took another sip of wine.

"Jane. Did something happen?"

"Marisol called last night." Jane filled her mother in on the conversation. Her mom had been the only person in the world Jane had confided in about her empty marriage. She'd talked it over with Mom first before she'd seen the divorce lawyer.

"Oh, honey, I'm so sorry."

"Yeah. Guess I didn't fool anybody after all. Was staying in my marriage for the kids really the right thing to do?" Jane had asked herself that a couple of thousand times, but she'd never asked her mom. Until now.

"You'll never know, Jane. You made a choice, and I supported you. And you were going to leave Stan. Does Marisol know that?"

"No. It's—" Jane stopped, unable to explain herself.

"You don't want to complicate the problem by giving Marisol even more information to fret about. I think that's good. She doesn't need to know the details. If she presses you further, tell her that nobody can know what goes on in a marriage except the two partners. And that you loved Stan."

Jane sighed.

"I know you did, honey. I was there." Mom patted Jane's hand.

Jane had been so very much in love. Stan was her world from the moment she met him. They dated all through college, but senior year, Stan dropped out when his father died so he could take over the family's manufacturing plant. He'd driven from Detroit to Ann Arbor every weekend to see Jane. They'd married the month she graduated with her BFA.

"Maybe I should say that the marriage had not been what I'd hoped for when I fell in love with Stanley. After all, it's true."

Her mom nodded, but the truth was Jane believed Stan was the one who had changed. He had not been there for her. The honeymoon period had lasted less than five years. Then he bailed. She'd tried to get him to talk to her, tried couple's therapy, but Stan said she was the unhappy one, so she could go to therapy on her own. In Stan's mind, unhappiness had always been her problem. Where had the guy gone who had been so in love with her that he couldn't wait for her to finish college to marry? Couldn't wait to start a family together? Never let go of her hand when they walked through a mall or down a street or into a restaurant? Never looked at her with less than adoration in his eyes? She hadn't conjured that Stan from her imagination. And she never knew, not really, where that guy had gone or why. Had she done something? When she'd asked, he'd refused to answer her. But maybe in time he'd have told her what went wrong. Now she'd never know.

Jane had stopped obsessing about this subject years ago, but Stan's death and Marisol's confrontation had brought it roaring back. "I guess I just wonder what happened. What made him change toward me? He would never say. Now he never will."

Her mom didn't answer right away. The server had appeared just as Jane stopped talking, so they passed a silent several minutes as the server asked if they'd like freshly ground pepper? No? Perhaps another glass of wine? Which was when Jane realized she'd finished her wine.

"No, thanks. Just water."

Finally the server left them to their food, and Jane ate, even though she still wasn't hungry.

"Your therapist at the time, did she explain that some men are unable to reconcile the woman they love with the mother of their children?"

"Yeah, she said some men, once they see how

21

messy childbirth is, they lose all sexual desire for their partner."

"It happens more often than you might think. But Jane," Mom said, "I wouldn't give Marisol any other information. Children do not need to know the details of their parents' relationship. Good or bad or somewhere in the middle."

Jane nodded and speared a chunk of iceberg lettuce. She loved how everything in Florida was kind of like when she was a kid back in Detroit. Classic rock played softly in grocery stores and restaurant menus always had a blue cheese wedge salad. They had the tiny slider burgers Jane remembered from when a quarter pound of ground beef seemed like a huge indulgent burger. Now in Detroit, the menus boasted half-pound burgers loaded with three kinds of cheese and topped with deep fried onion rings. You could get those things here, too, but people down here just didn't eat that way.

"The thing is, sometimes I am happy. Happier than I have been in a long, long time. Then I feel guilty about it, and I'm back to baseline," Jane admitted, although that wasn't quite accurate. Baseline was work, and Jane didn't work anymore. She had projects. Fixing up her home. Finding her way around the nooks and crannies and tiny art galleries of St. Pete. Buying a new wardrobe for a new climate. Making friends. Still, she didn't want to get into all that with Mom. Mom was happily retired. Jane didn't want to put her in the shrink chair again.

"What is baseline?" Mom asked.

"Not sure," Jane said. "I'm still figuring it out."

"You may have survivor's guilt," Mom said.

"Okay. Really?"

"Let's stop at the bookstore. I have a book I want you to read. When I get back from the cruise, we'll talk again."

Jane looked skeptical.

"Knowledge is power," Mom said.

"Yeah, okay, you're right. It's weird. I'm pissed off at a dead guy. Not sure they have a book for that."

"You need to find a new normal, honey. Paint. Write. Take up yoga."

Jane had been practicing yoga for thirty years. How depressing that her mom did not know that. She needed to share the positive stuff with her mom, not just bring her problems to solve.

"I'm sure I'll be fine," Jane said. It's what her mom wanted to hear and what Jane wanted to believe.

****

Jane texted Danny Saturday afternoon, after she'd read a little bit of the book her mom had recommended.

—Do you have a minute to talk?—

Her phone rang, and Danny's photo flashed.

"Hey, honey, thanks for calling."

"No problem. I was cleaning the bathroom and needed a break."

Her son was a good husband and a hard worker. He played as hard as he worked. But the stock markets were closed on the weekend, and Danny had always been able to turn off the math that ran through his mind like a peculiar poetry. It was a gift, many of Danny's teachers, even in elementary school, had claimed. She should encourage him. He should go to a prep school, then to Harvard. But Danny didn't want Harvard. He was interested in the intersection of computers and math. He wanted to write code that took the emotion out of choosing stocks. So he chose MIT and never looked back. He had Stan's dedication and focus as well as Jane's romantic dreaminess.

"Marisol, am I right?" he said.

"Yes. And I told her I am *not* happy your father died. It's a terrible tragedy."

"I know, Ma."

Jane supposed he did. His emotional intelligence was as sharp as all those other intelligences that made him brilliant at his job.

"Okay, honey, well, that's good."

"How're Gran and Pops?"

"Just fine. Going on a three-week cruise. How's Julie?"

"Wanting me to take her to brunch."

Jane heard Julie yell hello in the background.

"Tell her I love her, and take her to brunch."

"Will do. Love you too, Mom."

And that was it. Danny was loving and fully present for every moment of his life. Stan had not made it easy for Danny to step away from a family business that had been around since the invention of the automobile, but Danny never seemed to mind his father's brusque rhetoric. He knew his path from a very young age, and he set about pursuing it. When Stan died, Jane had sold his share in the family business to Stan's brother, then sent Danny and Marisol each half of the money.

Danny hadn't asked any of the hard questions Jane had been trying to find answers to in the pages of a book on complicated grief. Jane had been putting off this final grief around Stan. She'd mourned him, mourned the death of their relationship, for the last twenty years or so. She took out her sketchbook and drew his face. She hadn't seen it as often as she'd have liked, and when she did, he was usually asleep. When was the last time they'd looked each other in the eyes? Even more distant, when was the last time they'd looked at each other with love?

****

Sunday morning after the dance, Jane's body felt like she'd been assaulted with a bag of rocks. The band had been stellar. The ladies line-danced in perfect syncopation. Jane was more freestyle, but she decided to learn the steps to the line dances. Exercise and music were good for healing. So were friends. Queenie asked Jane about Waylon Silvercloud's yard and repeated her invitation that Jane come to art class soon. Jane said, "Maybe," thinking about how her dad had done what countless musicians did when they retired. They moved to Florida and played rock 'n' roll.

Jane had danced the night away with the widows, and now she was paying the price. Worth it, she decided, hobbling into her kitchen for coffee. Before she took her first sip, her doorbell rang, much louder than usual. She needed coffee and aspirin. But she dutifully went down the hall and peered into the tiny video camera at the front door.

George, her neighbor. She didn't know him well—he'd just moved in—but he was also from Detroit, so, despite his youth, which kicked her out of her position as youngest owner in Winding Bayou, she let him in. George didn't bat an eye at her cut-off jean shorts, baggy sleep shirt, or bed hair. Jane had to stop herself from trying to smooth down her rioting curls. She folded her arms across her shirt because she wasn't wearing a bra. He didn't notice. His eyes were wild with panic.

"What is it?" Jane motioned for him to come in and follow her down the hall. "Sorry. Late night. I need coffee."

She poured two cups and nodded to George to take one before she grabbed the aspirin bottle from the cupboard. She threw some pills down her throat and slurped a long sip of coffee. She was still waiting for George to speak. He had tried to lift his mug of coffee, but his hands trembled so violently that the coffee sloshed onto the countertop. She'd drained half her cup by this time, so she set it down and repeated her first words to him. "What the hell is wrong, George?"

He fell into a seat at the snack bar separating her galley kitchen from the sunroom. He gouged his eyes with the heels of his hands. "I don't know where to start," he moaned. "Okay. So. There is a very bloody shirt—it's dried blood—on the front seat of my car. There are a ton of cops outside the gate. Have you not heard the sirens?"

Jane didn't know much about George except he was very young, an early seasonal renter just in from Detroit. They'd seen each other in passing, and he'd seemed harmless enough.

"I had some trouble back in Detroit," he said, reaching into his back pocket and pulling out his wallet.

Relief released the breath Jane hadn't noticed she was holding. For a second, she'd thought George might be going for a gun. Which was stupid because why would he come to her house and tell her about a bloody shirt in his car only to shoot her?

"What kind of trouble?" Jane was not sure she wanted to know the answer.

George pulled a business card out of the wallet and handed it to Jane.

Jane scanned the card with wobbly vision. Barbara Stone. Special Agent. FBI. What?

"If the cops come for me, and I have no doubt they will, would you please call that number and tell Barb I need her?"

"Okay." Jane tucked the card into her shorts and moved George's half-empty coffee mug over to him at the bar. She kept her position in the galley kitchen across from him. They drank some coffee.

"Where did the bloody shirt come from, George?"

"I have no fucking idea. Honest. To. God." George drew in a deep breath. "I helped Barb put a mob of Detroit bad guys in prison. Made a deal with the Feds. I worked for these criminals, but small-time stuff. They'd give me stolen credit cards, and I'd go into luxury stores and buy purses or jewelry for my wife and daughters. I didn't have a wife, or any kids; it was the story I fed Barb when she was posing undercover as a sales clerk at the mall."

Jane tried to filter this information into a story that explained the bloody shirt. She couldn't.

"So, that play worked a bunch of times until finally I got caught and did the deal with the FBI to testify against my bosses. What they did was sell the stolen goods at pop-up stalls in the city. It was a sweet little scheme and worked really well for over a year. I was just a small-time crook. But turns out my bosses had lots of other things they were selling. Drugs. Girls."

Jane's spine straightened as the aspirin, and maybe

anxiety, kicked in. This did not sound good.

"I didn't know about the human trafficking! I only did the credit-card scam. I was good at it. Like an acting job. I played a wealthy married man. Anyway, Barb thought I could help them, do like a sting, because of my acting skills, so I flipped. I turned on the crooks; I set them up. As I said, they were into some very bad stuff. Which I didn't know about, just want to reiterate."

Jane still didn't see any connection to a bloody shirt in George's front seat.

"The shirt, George."

"Oh. Yeah. Well, I was on my run around the bayou trail this morning, and I saw a swarm of cop cars down on Orange Blossom. They got the road blocked off and a tent all around one area and an ambulance backed up to it. You know, how the cops do so people don't put photos on the internet."

"Photos of what?" Jane didn't know, but she was starting to worry. Orange Blossom. Cops. Ambulance. Waylon.

"Pictures of murder victims." George finished his coffee and set the mug down. "You got anything stronger?"

Jane looked in her liquor cabinet. "Brandy? Bourbon? Vodka?" Jane didn't drink bourbon, so that bottle was full. George chose the bourbon.

"Rocks?"

"Naw."

She poured his bourbon neat. She pushed it toward him across the bar, then made herself another coffee. She debated adding a shot of brandy, but her queasy stomach from the many glasses of wine she'd consumed the night before said absolutely not.

She took her coffee into the sunroom, which looked out over the main street of Winding Bayou. She opened her blinds with a flick of the remote. The entire wall was windows; she could see clear down to the clubhouse and past that to Orange Blossom Avenue. The street curved a bit just past Waylon's place, but the roadblock, tent, and cop cars were all still there. She couldn't be sure at which house they had gathered. She sat on one of two small sofas in the sunroom. George came around and sat on the other one, a large glass table with a dark wicker base between them. When George set down his crystal goblet, she noticed he'd already finished the bourbon. She got up and brought the bottle to the table. He poured another drink. It couldn't have been much after ten a.m.

"So…are you thinking the bloody shirt is connected to whatever is happening on Orange Blossom?"

"I'm afraid it is. I'm not sure, but why the fuck would someone put a bloody shirt in my vehicle?"

"Are you sure it's blood?"

"Even if it's not, it's meant to look like blood. I think someone in the Detroit mob is sending me a message. I just hope to hell that shirt does not belong to a murdered man."

That was another big jump in logic, but this time Jane could read George's thoughts.

"A man's shirt? What did it look like? How large was it?" Waylon was a large man. The day she'd seen him, he'd worn a plaid flannel shirt with the sleeves cut off.

"It was so covered in blood I really couldn't tell.

And I didn't touch it. I'm not that stupid."

Jane was sure of only one thing. "You have to call the police."

"I know. I'm going to. I just wanted to give you Barb's number so you could fill her in on what's happening if they lock me up."

"I have no idea what's happening, George."

"That makes two of us."

Jane believed him.

"Just tell her I need her help and explain everything I said to you."

Jane nodded.

George pulled his cell phone out of his front pocket. Jane put the bourbon bottle away while he was connected to the police. She tried to memorize what he said.

"My name is George Sanders, I live in unit 202 in Winding Bayou, and I found a bloody shirt in my car this morning." He said "no" a couple of times and then hung up.

By the time Jane realized George lived in 201 and her unit was 202, someone was pounding on the door and shouting, "Open up. Police." They must have peeled off from the action on Orange Blossom to get here so fast.

"I'm sorry about all this," George said. "Call Barb, okay?"

* * * *

Jane waited until George had shut the storm door behind him. When no further knocking or demands to open up ensued, she texted Kim.

—*Is Waylon okay?*—

Last night at the dance, Kim had talked a lot about

Waylon. She'd been back to see him a few times, and a romance had begun to simmer between them. Then she remembered Kim had a doctor's appointment this morning. When Kim didn't respond to her text, Jane figured she'd probably muted her phone. How were people getting in and out of Winding Bayou? Had Kim seen the chaos on Orange Blossom Avenue, or did she get out before the action started?

From her sunroom, Jane could see Bayou folk gathering at the gate and some walking toward the activity on Orange Blossom. She needed a shower. Then she'd walk down there herself. On the way, she'd find out if George was still home or if he'd been hauled down to the cop shop.

****

Jane did not get a chance to walk down to Orange Blossom. Nor did she have the opportunity to check on George. After she'd showered and dressed and somewhat tamed her hair, her door bell chimed again. Damn that George for giving her unit number instead of his own. She walked down the hall, which seemed longer than ever, and saw a badge held up to her doorbell camera. She turned on the intercom system and said, "Yes?"

"Detective Singer, St. Petersburg Police Department. Jane Chasen?"

She opened the storm door, saw a gorgeous man, almost as good-looking as her neighbor George, but more her age. She was glad, despite circumstances, that she'd taken five minutes to apply makeup after her shower. At the same time, she berated herself for being so frivolous. Something bad had happened. She needed to take it seriously.

"Yes, I'm Jane." She spoke through the screen door. Handsome detective Singer had a female officer in uniform with him. He was in the process of slipping his wallet into the back pocket of shell-colored linen slacks. His impeccable linen shirt was loose enough to camouflage his weapon. She stared maybe a minute too long, hadn't seen men's shirts like this in Detroit. There, guys wore concert T-shirts, casual golf shirts, or white button-downs with suit and tie. She blinked in approval at his casual elegance. She moved her eyes up before her glance at toned biceps turned into a stare. The shirt was like something a movie star might wear on a yacht. It flowed loosely except at the sleeves where it clung to his tanned muscular biceps. Damn. This never happened to her. She hadn't even wanted to have an affair when Stan cut off sex. That hadn't changed since she'd been a widow. And now here she was, trying not to drown in this cop's Tampa Bay blue eyes.

Chapter Three

"How can I help you?"

"We'd like to ask you a few questions." Detective Singer motioned to the female cop. "This is Officer Patrice Riley."

Jane, not having been questioned by the police since Stan's accidental death, wasn't sure of the procedure. "Would you like to come in?" she finally asked, not opening the door until he nodded yes. Again the walk down the long hall.

"Nice mural," said Officer Patrice Riley. Patrice. An unusual name. She liked the way it sounded.

"Thanks," Jane said, over her shoulder.

Jane had found an artist in Largo who painted a mermaid swimming toward her kitchen down the long length of one hallway wall. Stan would never have allowed any such décor, but the mermaid thrilled Jane. Everything she'd done here, from her pink galley kitchen and watermelon wine glasses to the antique cocktail trolley in the sunroom to the oasis of her ocean blue bedroom, thrilled Jane. She liked the white Cindy Crawford sofa in the living room just fine, too. She gestured to it and asked them if they'd like anything to drink. That's what the people in the British mysteries she liked to read did when the cops came to call.

"No," said Singer, unlike the British police, who always said yes. Patrice stayed silent, checking out

Jane's décor, not bothering to hide her interest. Jane had worked hard on making this home a reflection of her truest self, so she smiled at Patrice despite the grim situation almost certainly looming.

Jane sat in her favorite chair, but not because it was closest to Singer, who had taken up the left side of the sofa and was flipping through a notebook. Jane arranged her features into a less frivolous expression, hoping Singer had not seen her smile as Patrice clocked the Frida Kahlo self-portrait, the one with a monkey on Frida's shoulder that Jane had picked up downtown.

Singer asked Jane about her recent move to Florida. Why had she left Detroit? What had landed her here? "Be brief. I'll stop you if I want more detail." Patrice handed Singer a sharpened pencil she'd taken from her shirt pocket.

Jane gathered her thoughts. "My husband died. My parents live here. My kids live in Seattle and New York. They have their own careers and families. I did not want to stay in Detroit, but I couldn't move to Seattle or New York. That would be like playing favorites, right?"

So far, Detective Singer hadn't written anything down.

"When did your husband die?" he asked.

"Not quite six months ago." She shivered even though it was warm in the condo. "He died in our house. I found him when I returned from a business trip. He'd been dead, electrocuted, for a few days. I knew as soon as I walked in the door something was wrong. I sold the house as quickly as I could and came here. I hung out with Mom and Dad all hurricane season; my mom and I did a lot of shopping for the condo. We'd meet up with Dad for dinner at the club after his daily golf game. Then in October, I flew to Seattle to check in with my daughter and spend some time with my granddaughter. I went to New York, too, where my son and his wife live. Stan's death was hard on my kids." Detective Singer didn't have to know exactly how difficult Stan's unexpected death had been on Marisol and Danny. "My parents just left on a Mediterranean cruise." She had to stop thinking about Marisol's FaceTime call last week.

Jane knew things had tumbled out a bit helter-skelter and that she'd probably said more than she needed to about her family. But Singer had remained silent, only the sound of his pencil scratching notes came from the Cindy Crawford sofa.

Next, Singer went through all the things Jane expected he would: why George had given her address and not his own, how well she knew him, what George had said to her this morning. The business card from FBI Barb burned a hole in Jane's pocket, but she didn't mention that. She did tell Singer that George had been upset about a bloody shirt in his car. "He said he didn't know how it got there and that he never touched it."

After that, Singer asked yet another question she hadn't expected.

"Did you and George know each other back in Detroit?"

"No, of course not! He's twenty years younger than I am." Jane elaborated. "And we don't exactly hang out with the same crowd. I was a wife and mother and had a busy career. I traveled for my job. Our paths never crossed, and why would they? But he did tell me about his criminal history just this morning."

"So you only learned of his background today?"

"Most of it, yes. He'd told me in passing that he was from Detroit. I had on a ball cap one time when he was going up the stairs and I was coming down. So he said, "Hey, Big D," or something like that, and we chatted for a few minutes, right there in the stairwell. This morning, I guess he panicked. He asked me to contact his FBI support person, Barb. That was the main reason he came by. He had a feeling the police would arrest him…Did you? Arrest him?"

"No," Singer said. He flipped his notebook shut and stood. Done. He didn't ask more about Detroit. He didn't mention Barb. Patrice sighed and rose along with Singer. Jane had a feeling Patrice had liked the sofa.

Jane got up too. "Listen. I have a friend, well, more of an acquaintance, really, on Orange Blossom Avenue. Waylon Silvercloud. I saw the commotion down there from the sunroom windows this morning. Is Waylon okay?"

"No comment." Singer might be good-looking, but he was all business. It reminded her a little of Stan. She shivered again. Hoped she wasn't coming down with a cold. Probably nothing more than wine flu.

"I'll just Google it." She picked up her phone from the end table where her latest British mystery novel was splayed. She wondered if reading murder mysteries made her look suspicious. Her hands shook a little bit. She had a bad feeling. She really didn't want to know if it was Waylon's bloody shirt in George's car. She didn't check her phone, because she didn't want Singer to see her hands shake. She kept it in her hand at her side.

Singer didn't respond to her Google threat, but he

didn't leave, either.

She didn't want to say another word, but her mouth had other ideas. "Listen. I'm an art lecturer. Well, retired. But anyway, I liked his yard installation and told him so earlier this past week when I walked over to check it out." She decided not to mention Kim. She didn't want to drag her friend into this drama for no good reason.

"Yard installation?" Singer asked.

"An art installation is a physical space made into art. He did that with his yard."

"So did Waylon tell you he was an artist?"

"No. But he wouldn't. He's an outsider artist. You know, not connected to the art world. Not trained. Not trying to get famous. Just doing his own thing. For his own pleasure. Or maybe it was a kind of obsession. You must have heard of Simon Rodia? Watts Towers? L.A.?"

Singer appeared stymied. For some reason, Jane found this satisfying. If he didn't know Rodia, she wouldn't bother mentioning Guyton's Heidelberg Project in Detroit. Those were the two outsider artists she'd been asked to lecture on most often. Singer didn't speak for a long moment. Patrice had wandered over to the watermelon wine glasses displayed on the antique cocktail trolley.

"Do you have a forensic artist at your PD?" From her mystery reading, Jane knew forensic artists, formerly known as sketch artists, worked for law enforcement all over the world.

"No," Singer said.

"You might not need one. If Waylon is okay. If nobody's messed with his yard."

"Why do you think someone has 'messed with his yard'?"

"Oh, I don't. I hope not. It's just, people around here thought he was a junk collector or a hoarder or something. They didn't see Waylon as an artist like someone with a trained eye would."

"Someone like you?"

"Well, yeah." She wasn't bragging. It was just a fact. "I know art like you know police work."

Her phone, still in her hand, dinged, signaling an incoming message. Kim. Jane lifted the screen to her face and read *Someone killed Waylon.*

Jane's hands were shaking even harder than before. She didn't try to text. She used the microphone to send an audio text back to Kim. She spoke into the phone: "Police are here. I'll explain later." She watched the screen to make sure her words came out right, then sent the text.

"Oh my God," Jane said immediately after she sent the text. "Somebody did kill him!" She took a deep breath. What would happen to Waylon's life's work? It would be the worst sort of tragedy if the police hauled it all away and kept it locked up in some dusty evidence room. "Is his yard intact?"

"We can't say." Singer's jaw muscles tensed. His face had such good lines. Strong jawline, smooth skin, unflinching clear eyes that looked directly into hers without hesitation. The kind of features ancient sculptors worked lifetimes to capture in marble. But marble was cold, Jane reminded herself. She needed to finish reading that book her mother recommended about complicated grief. Could there be an explanation for why, suddenly, when an artist she'd just discovered had been found dead, she kept picturing a police detective without his shirt on? Was she fragmenting, focusing on a long-dormant emotional response as a way to be in denial about death? And was it Waylon's death or Stan's she was really upset about? Could it be both? It had to be both.

She made herself stop ruminating. Waylon's yard. Had any part of it been damaged? Why wouldn't Singer tell her? She pressed him. "Can't or won't?"

"Can't. We don't know what it looked like before his death." He had seemed to give up on not telling her anything, at least where Waylon was concerned. But he'd said *death*, not *murder*.

Jane checked her phone. The photos Kim had sent her, a dozen close shots of the various art forms in Waylon's yard installation, were there on a file. Jane hadn't known why she'd saved them. She was trying to find her footing, was all. Art was familiar. Maybe she had some kind of vague idea about studying Waylon's works in more depth. Maybe she'd try to score an interview or document the man and his work in a recording. Maybe she just wanted to be his friend. But that was before someone had killed him.

She should show the photos to Singer. She knew that. But she wanted to protect Kim, too. What to do?

"Who texted you just now?" Singer asked.

"A neighbor. Seems like everyone here knows Waylon was murdered."

Singer did not confirm or deny.

He started toward the hallway, Patrice on his heels. Jane followed them to the door, furiously rushing to hatch a plan. She followed them outside. They were halfway to the stairwell when she said, "Detective

Singer?"

He turned to her. Then he said something to Patrice, and she continued down the stairs toward the squad car while he walked back toward Jane. She distrusted the thrill that shot from her tailbone up her spine. Get a grip, she told herself. Maybe she'd get the audio version of that grief book. Maybe she'd find a therapist. But first, she was going to show Singer the photos, that was it. He wouldn't know that she hadn't taken them herself.

She stood by the railing in front of her porch area. Singer joined her there. They were in the shade, so the pictures were pretty clear. She kept the phone in her hand as she went through them, letting him get a good look at each of the ten photos.

"Waylon knew about these photos, and he knew I was interested in his work." All true. "I'm happy to send you these."

He pulled a card out of his wallet and handed it to her. His official police email address was on it. "Send them here," he said. "Don't leave town, okay?" Jane knew cops often said that to people after a crime was committed, but it spooked her anyway. What if Marisol needed her? What if Danny did? Who was she kidding? Those kids hadn't needed her for a long time now.

"I wasn't planning on it."

"Good."

"But why not? I'm not a suspect, am I?"

Singer laughed before he caught himself. Damn him. Was he trying to be charming and enigmatic? "Ah, no," he said. "I was thinking about what you said about a forensic artist. I can get the guy Seminole County uses, but I think we may need somebody with a different set of skills."

Jane caught her breath. "Me?"

"Maybe. Would you be interested in answering some art-related questions if the occasion arises?"

"Sure." She needed her heart to behave. "I still have a website if you want to check out my credentials."

"Yes. Patrice looked you up on the way over."

So half of what she told him, or more, probably more, he'd already known.

She sent him the file anyway and heard his phone buzz through his shirt pocket. "That'll be the photos, Detective Singer." She tried to keep her voice and her expression professional. Lord knows she had years of practice hiding her feelings.

"Thanks." He nodded once, turned, and walked away.

She did not check out his ass. Not on purpose, anyway.

She walked back inside, texting Kim.

****

Turned out the police had interviewed Kim already. They'd found her fingerprints all over Waylon's house. But Kim didn't know any more than Jane about how Waylon had died or if the shirt George had found was Waylon's. George, in fact, did not know this either. Both Kim and George were scared to death that they were suspects.

Jane found all this out as they met in front of the building five minutes after Singer and Patrice had left in a squad car. The three of them started walking down toward Waylon's. Jane admitted she'd given Singer the photos of his yard, and Kim said that was fine.

41

Jane started to introduce George and Kim, but Kim already knew George from the pool. They both had great tans. "George puts sunscreen on my shoulders," Kim said.

"I would never have met Kim if it wasn't for the pool," George said. "I'm not the type to come to a coffee at the clubhouse and, excuse me, but the kind of music they play at the dances is not my thing."

"Who doesn't like classic rock?" Kim said.

"Me," George said. "Jane, did the cops mention anything about the bloody shirt? They had me give them a DNA sample."

Kim stopped walking; her face paled and she swayed a little, standing there. Both Jane and George rushed to hold her up, but Kim shook her head. "I'm fine. I just—This is the first time I'm hearing about the shirt."

"The police removed it from my car, where some unknown person placed it. They put it in an evidence bag," he said. "They impounded my car, too."

"So are you going to call your FBI friend?" Jane asked.

"Not unless they arrest me," George said, after they'd filled Kim in on that part of the story. "She's already got me stereotyped as a slimeball."

"And you really like her," Kim guessed.

"Yep," George confirmed.

"I really liked Waylon," Kim said. "You sure you didn't kill him?"

"Don't you think the cops would have arrested me if I had? They got my DNA, so that the lab can rule me out as placing the shirt there. They reviewed the video footage of the passageway on the second floor. Proof I went into the condo at midnight and didn't come out until I went for my run this morning. But to answer your question, no. I didn't kill the guy. Okay?"

Kim sniffed. "He was such a nice man."

Jane wanted to talk to Kim about Waylon, about how Kim had been able to move on from her husband's death. But it wouldn't be kind, and Kim had not had the same kind of troubled marriage Jane had endured. She reminded herself not to think about Stan or the past. She was moving forward.

They passed the clubhouse and were coming up to the gate. The police were still there and some neighbors stood around, but the crowd had thinned since earlier this morning. The tent clearly surrounded Waylon's yard and even his fencing around the property. It went all the way up to the house on both sides. Jane had an image of Waylon's body being pierced by the sharp points of the iron gate. She needed to switch from mystery to romance novels. How would someone get Waylon, a very large man, onto his gate? Her imagination was in overdrive. Then she saw Mary, Waylon's neighbor. The lady who had brought him meatloaf sandwiches the day Kim and Jane had met the artist.

The three Winding Bayou residents stopped a bit short of walking up to Waylon's home, still blocked from view by a police tent.

"Kim, did you get to know Mary any better?" Jane asked.

Mary stood next to a short wiry guy in board shorts and a tank top. He was barefoot. He had to reach up to put his arm around Mary's shoulder.

"Yeah, a bit. That's Pip with her. Mary and

Waylon are Wind Clan. People in the same clan have brother and sister relationships. Pip is Creek. He's not Mary's boyfriend or anything, but they're the only three Native Americans on the block, so they're tight. Well, Waylon didn't care for Pip, but he put up with him for Mary's sake."

"Yo, Kim," Pip yelled.

Several people turned to see who Pip was addressing.

"Shit," Kim said.

"What?" Jane asked. Jane felt a tug as Kim pulled on the crook of her elbow.

"Listen. That Pip guy was no fan of Waylon's. He was jealous of Mary and Waylon's close relationship."

"Well, okay," Jane said. "I'll keep that in mind." She took Kim's hand off her arm and patted it. "Would you rather we didn't go any farther?"

"No. No. Let's go on. I want to give Mary a hug. She's really nice, and she loved Waylon." Kim's voice trembled. She seemed about to cry, but then she straightened her spine and continued her story. "I just want you to know that the neighbors mostly thought Waylon was crazy. He drank a lot and howled at full moons."

Jane knew about the thin line between art and madness. It wasn't a secret that many creative types were more than a little quirky. As much as Jane admired artists, she'd never wanted to be one. Too many of them had tortured souls.

"I admire Waylon's work. And I met him, too. He wasn't mental patient material. Just maybe had a few too many when the moon was full?"

Kim chuckled. "Yeah, guess that's right."

They moved down the street toward Mary and Pip and whoever else was still gawking. As they got closer, they had to sidestep the flowers strewn on either side of the police tarp. Pictures of Waylon were pinned to a makeshift altar, with candles burning around his images. Most everyone there was Indian. The haters had moved on. One St. Pete police officer was on duty at the front of the tarp. Tribal police acted as guards as they talked easily to the group of mourners. The Seminole Nation had a powerful presence in Florida. They owned a huge casino in Tampa, sharing the wealth by funding Native American museums and other Indian public services. Jane was relieved they were there, on duty, to protect Waylon's legacy.

"Mary," Jane said after Kim's long hug was over. "I'm so sorry for your loss."

Pip spat in the street. "Who's this white bitch?"

Mary ignored him. Jane tried to do that, too, but she one hundred percent understood why Waylon had not liked Pip.

"You remember Jane, Mary. She was with me on that first day, when you brought Waylon his lunch."

Mary nodded. "The art lecturer," she said.

Jane hadn't told Waylon or Mary what she'd done for a living. She glanced at Kim, who smiled like an innocent angel.

"I want to introduce you to Waylon's family," Mary said, moving into a knot of Indians.

Kim and Jane followed. Pip stayed behind. Good.

"I never met the family," Kim whispered to Jane.

The eldest woman in the knot of Waylon's relatives shook Jane's hand, then Kim's. "Thank you for appreciating my son's work. It means a lot to the family. His sisters"—she waved at two women about Mary's age—"the entire Wind Clan, and all of the Seminole Nation thank you."

No applause after a lecture had ever moved Jane as much. She was speechless. Kim's voice, however, was in fine working order.

Kim said, "I shot extensive photos of the installation. We don't know yet if any of the Work has been messed with"—Kim definitely said work with a capital W—"but Jane will be able to tell you once the police bring her in to consult on the case." Kim knew more than Jane did about that, but the grateful expression on Mrs. Silvercloud's face kept Jane mum.

"Oh, will you let us know? They have not even let the family inside that tent," one of Waylon's sisters said. Jane wondered if they were biological sisters or Wind Clan sisters. It didn't matter. They'd all loved Waylon and were all aware of his talent.

"I'm not sure when, or if, I'll be allowed inside, but let me get your contact information," Jane said. She knew what she was going to do next. She was going to go home and work up descriptions of Waylon's various groupings of art. With slides. And then she'd present it to his family. Maybe she'd send Singer a copy. She knew she was good at her job, but this wasn't about impressing some handsome cop. It was about preserving Waylon's legacy for his family, his Clan, and the Seminole Nation.

Maybe there would be a way the influential Seminoles could keep Waylon's installation intact.

When Kim and Jane finally left the site, Pip yelled something about useless white women, but Kim said, "Ignore him," so Jane did. He'd probably turn out to be

Waylon's murderer. Jane needed to remember to tell Detective Singer about the conflict between Pip and Waylon next time she saw him. If there was a next time.

Chapter Four

At the end of a long day at her laptop, Jane sat in her sunroom watching the sun go down behind the palm trees lining the boulevard. The solar blaze bathed the buff-colored buildings in topaz light. Seeing it change to a peach blush was so exquisite Jane didn't mind not being at the beach with the showy shades of pink, orange, and lavender. Beach sunsets were fine, but the understated display in Jane's sunroom was nice, too.

She'd sent her finished project to Waylon's mom and to Singer. She'd sent a copy to Kim, too. After all, they were Kim's photos. She deserved to know how they'd been used. In the opening remarks before the descriptions, Jane had been short on biography, no mention of his murder, which would make it better for the family. She spent her time on the art descriptions, and they were solid. She'd been thinking about Waylon and his yard for a long time. Almost since the day she first drove down Orange Blossom Avenue and spotted glimmers from the corner of her eye. It felt good to release all that thinking into a familiar form. It would not have happened without Kim's photographs.

"Alexa," Jane said, "play 'If You Could Read My Mind' by Gordon Lightfoot." The band had played the old song for a slow dance last night. It had reminded Jane of her long marriage and her anguish before she accepted the limits of the union. She didn't know where their love went or why it left, and though she'd tried, she could never get it back. The song summed it up. Why Stan preferred work to family, to love, was a mystery he'd taken to his grave.

Marisol condemned Jane, and as a mother, that hurt. But she'd gotten a chance to read a little more from the grief book and turned out, lots of families had difficulties accepting a member's death. Especially if that family member had been troublesome or mostly absent from the family circle.

"Admit it. You're glad he's dead," Marisol had said on FaceTime, her tired eyes full of anger. The force of it had almost knocked Jane down. Now it wanted to hit her again. But Jane was tired of thinking and rethinking. Waylon's murder had jolted her out of her own head. She'd enjoyed capturing Waylon's installation, using words to describe what he made.

Her daughter believed what she needed to believe. It wasn't true, but the truth wouldn't help. How she'd wanted to leave Stan a hundred times, how she'd saved up the idea of divorce for so many years, the way other couples saved for an idyllic retirement full of travel and renewed closeness after a lifetime of building a family.

Jane would have never wished Stan dead. Never. It was horrible that his life had been cut short. Jane was sorry for that. Sorry she wasn't closer to Marisol, that when Jane had texted her the title of the book on grief, her daughter had sent an angry-face emoji instead of calling her and talking things out. She'd only seen her daughter's emoji after she'd stopped working for the day.

Jane used to wonder if the kids thought they were the reason Stan worked so much. She hoped not. At least for right now, Marisol considered Jane guilty. That was okay. It would be worse if Marisol thought her father's behavior had anything to do with herself. Jane could take the hit. For now. At some point, she'd need to resolve things with Marisol. She wouldn't give up on her daughter's love the way she'd given up on Stan. She'd never stop fighting for a loving relationship with Marisol, but she would give her daughter some more time to process things in her own way. And she'd tried not to guilt trip too much.

But she'd thought about blame and how much was hers. How she and Stan were both so caught up in their careers, more than was probably healthy. How she only started traveling out of state after the kids were in college. Had that been why Stan had seen no reason to stop his crazy work schedule? Would he have tried harder if she'd been there more? Had she made it clear to him there would be no wife at home after the kids were gone? Well, she had. But it hadn't felt that way. It felt like she'd finally been able to come to terms with the shitty partnership fate had handed her. How she'd stuck out a sad situation to make life better for the kids, for herself. Family intact.

Jane wanted more than anything in that moment to talk to her own mother. Mom would put Marisol's nasty text into a context Jane could accept.

"It's the stages of grief, honey," Jane could hear her mother say. "Grief, anger, denial. Sounds like they've got some overlapping in there, but the point is, they're processing Stan's death, each in their own way. And yes, Marisol is probably projecting some of her anger and denial onto you." Was that Mom or something she'd read in the book?

Well, it was what her mom would say. It's what the grief book said, too. Her mom and dad knew she and Stan hadn't loved each other. That they'd only stayed together for the kids. It was pretty obvious. They didn't exactly exude affection in the few times they'd both been at family gatherings, like Thanksgiving. Stan closed his shop on Thanksgiving and Christmas, and some years, those were the only two days he took off.

Just give it some time, the grief book said. Try to live in the present moment. Start your life anew.

Jane tried to take that advice. She had succeeded for most of the day. But now her daughter's words haunted her as the house and the world darkened around her. She turned on a lamp and drew the shades. She didn't ask Alexa to play any more songs but sat in the quiet until her phone rang.

Jane checked caller ID. Jesse Singer. Singer's first name was Jesse!

"Hello, Jesse Singer," she said, before she could think better of it.

"Hey. I wanted to thank you for those detailed descriptions of the yard."

"I sent a copy to Waylon's mom, too. And one to Kim. They were actually her photos." Jane wondered if Singer remembered she had not told him Kim had taken the photos. "I didn't tell you they were Kim's pictures because I didn't want to drag her into anything. But then I found out you had already questioned her."

"Where'd you meet Waylon's mother?" Singer skipped over her stumbled backtracking. Jane guessed that meant he forgave her. Whew. She wanted him to like her. Something inside her insisted. Was this what moving forward felt like?

"Waylon's mom was at a kind of memorial outside that ugly tent you guys erected. Kim, George, and I went down there after you left this morning." Shit. She'd called his police tent ugly. "About the tent, it's a good ugly tent...I mean, it's good that it's there. And the guards. Will you have someone there 24-7?" Jane wanted to keep him talking, and also she wanted to hang up immediately because she sounded like an idiot.

"Tribal police are taking care of guard duty. Seminoles found out the yard was an important artifact before we did."

"It's good you're working together."

"Yes, and thank you for your help."

"My pleasure." Jane tried not to gush. Be professional, she told herself.

"Are you still up for helping us discern whether the yard has been tampered with?" Singer asked.

"Sure, Detective Singer." Jane squashed down the outrageous enthusiasm of her beating heart. Was this some kind of reaction to her lousy marriage and Marisol's disdain? He was not feeling the way she did right now. He was taking a shot at establishing motive, that was all. He was just doing his job. It wasn't like he was going to ask her on a date.

"I like how your voice sounded when you called me Jesse," he said.

Did she imagine a touch of warmth in his tone? It had not been there earlier, she was convinced. Would delusions be symptomatic of grief that was way more complicated than one word could sum up? She hoped the book had an index. She'd need to keep herself together. Not act like a silly teenager with a crush.

"Oh. Okay, Jesse. And you call me Jane." What the

heck, they were colleagues now. Had he been calling her Jane all along? She didn't remember.

"Will you meet me at ten a.m. at the site?"

"Yes. Happy to help."

She disconnected, wondering what one wore to consult on a murder investigation.

****

By ten a.m., she had showered and washed her hair. She had blown it dry and styled it with a flat iron, then pulled it back and secured it with a pretty clip. It took her thirty minutes, but she told herself she'd be leaning over plants and didn't need her hair in the way. Then she chose an outfit of cropped jeans and a navy T-shirt. Her practical side knew she'd likely be kneeling in dirt. Her new wardrobe of floaty sundresses would not work in this situation. Neither would two layers of mascara, but she applied them anyway.

She threw a jewel loupe and a magnifying glass into her large tote bag. She debated, then added her iPad. She locked up and went down to her car, then decided to walk. Maybe the exercise would settle the butterflies fluttering in her stomach like she was fifteen instead of fifty-five. She'd been twenty-five when she had her daughter and Stan had started working longer hours. For the kids, he'd said. And it was true. Kids cost money. College cost money. Soon they'd had two children and more expenses.

So at first, Stan working seven days from early morning until long into the night seemed sensible. Jane started to question that crazy work schedule when Stan refused to take vacations. Gradually, Jane realized Stan had not been present; Stan had been detached from their shared life. She was both mother and father to her kids, at least on an emotional level. And physically, too. Jane tried to talk to Stan about slowing down, but he had a short fuse, something that had not been there when she'd married him. He'd cut her off with a scathing comment and only communicated to the kids with rote replies. She stayed for the kids. For the financial security. For the insurance. For the appearance of a normal family.

Once the kids needed her less, she channeled all her passion into work. Now here she was, feeling juicy and so alive. Something was happening. It was different from anything she'd felt for what? Twenty years?

Wasn't menopause supposed to curtail desire? But Kim still felt desire, she'd felt it for Waylon and she'd known him less than a week. The couples at the dance had clung close like they were still in love. The widows at her table had all said they were open to a relationship, that they wanted one. There just weren't a whole lot of choices at Winding Bayou. Even Rich refused to come to the dance, despite his clear infatuation with Kim.

She admitted it. She was attracted to Jesse. Did he feel it too? Maybe. She'd been out of the game way too long to know for sure.

Before she knew it, she was at Waylon's mailbox. One of the tribal policemen on guard duty led her into the backyard, where Jesse waited. A large shed toward the back of the fenced property was painted the same red as the house. Waylon's work studio, she guessed. Jesse opened the back door, gesturing her inside so quickly she barely got a glimpse of the large backyard. From what she could see at a glance, the effusive greenery grew wild and unadorned by any of Waylon's art.

Jesse followed her inside a small kitchen outfitted with basic necessities: a white oven and stovetop, a scarred maple table and two chairs, no flourishes. Apparently, the fridge outside was the only one Waylon had owned.

"Thanks for doing this," Jesse said.

"I'm happy to help." Jane continued assessing the artist's abode but then sucked in a breath. Where on this property had Waylon died?

"What?" Jesse asked. Well, he was a detective. He read people's body language for a living, which was why he continued, unfazed. "The body was not discovered in the house."

"Where, then?" Jane asked, still thinking of the sharp points on Waylon's fencing. But how could anyone—no, she needed to ban that image.

"This is need-to-know," Jesse said.

"I'm not going to tell Kim or George. Or anyone." Jane's eyes met Jesse's. She hoped he saw that she was being truthful. The eyes never lied. At least according to her beloved British mystery novels.

"No, of course you won't," Jesse said. "He was found in the backyard, inside his work shed."

Jane felt there was something Jesse was holding back. That was okay. Need-to-know, etc. But she had to ask. "Was he stabbed with a wrought-iron gate post?"

Jesse couldn't quite keep his poker face. His eyebrows peaked. "Good guess," he said, not confirming or denying.

Jane didn't press him, further. At one time in her life, she might have done so. Not now. Not here. The Florida air changed a person. It had changed Jane.

There were days she didn't recognize herself. Today was one of them.

"I thought we'd start with the house; just walk with me and see what you notice. I'll record your observations for the record." He handed Jane gloves and shoe covers.

She didn't need to touch anything. The rest of the small home was as neat and minimal as the kitchen had been. There were no tools of the artist's trade, no brushes or paints, no magazines or books, no art or photographs on the walls, each room painted the same unassuming adobe color.

She sensed the real clues to Waylon's outsider persona would be in the workshop. His beading was particularly intriguing. Hand-blown high-quality glass. Did he blow the glass himself? She suspected he did, but his workshop would show proof. And who supplied his glass? She wondered whether she'd find sheets of it in the shed that would name the supplier.

They went through the front door of the house directly into the tent. Several strong standing lights kept the plants alive, if not exactly flourishing. There was a guard inside as well, but he left when she and Jesse came out of the house. She could hear the guard who'd escorted her back talking to the tent guard but didn't try to make out what they were saying. Her eyes were already plotting a careful path through the installation.

Five hours later, Jane and Jesse had finished inspecting every leaf on every plant, every side of each sculpture, every string of lustrous glass beads. They'd accounted for every single rod of wrought iron. They'd even pondered at the insides of Waylon's motor-oil-streaked refrigerator. It was empty. "There were a couple bags of food," Jesse said. "We took it in for analysis." He pointed to the tiny freezer. "There were two trays of ice and some mini-vodkas in there. Anything strike you as artsy?"

She smiled at Jesse's word choice. "Maybe Waylon drank vodka when he howled at the moon. But otherwise, no, just a fridge. An old one."

Jesse closed the fridge, and they stood under the carport next to the cherry red Harley.

"This is a Sportster," Jane said. "It doesn't announce itself like a Hog. It's sleeker. Like the house, everything suggests the taste of a man who saved his pleasure for the vibrancy and color reflected in his art."

Jane turned to again look at the installation, much the same as she had viewed it and as the photos reflected. Some expected disturbances, probably from wind, in the beaded glass strands close to the tent, some other bits of yard debris scattered here and there, likely related to the season. Every tip on the fence was still gilded as she'd originally seen. She had found nothing amiss, and that both pleased and dismayed her. Pleased for art's sake, disturbed because she'd wanted to uncover something for Jesse Singer, something that would make her a star in his eyes. Which was so stupid and made her feel like she was losing her grip on reality just a little bit. She needed to snap out of it.

"I hope he has glass-blowing tools in the shed out back."

"We can't check the shed," he said.

"Really?" Jane thought that if they'd find anything, that was the most likely place.

"Sorry. The body was found there and the weapon. Again—"

"Need to know. Got it." Jane followed the detective back through the house and around to the front yard.

"Did you walk down?" Jesse asked.

"I did."

"Want a ride home?"

"Yes." She hadn't felt any aches or pains up to that moment, but suddenly her back ached and her calf muscles cried. Or maybe she only noticed now because of that buzzy feeling that had followed her from her house all the way down to Waylon's place.

Jesse had an unmarked car. Dark sedan. Nondescript. Tidy but for several pencils of varying size and sharpness stuck inside the cup holder. They drove through the gates of the Bayou, each silent and in their own thoughts. She was a bit surprised when Jesse pulled into a parking space and insisted on seeing her to her door. Jane had a garage that led to an elevator, but she took the stair route, Jesse a step behind her.

She spotted George on the walkway. He was studying a postcard and didn't see them. Jane wished she'd asked Jesse how they'd cleared George of suspicion. Had it been the video footage like George had said? Why would George lie? And why was she so suspicious of everyone all of the sudden?

George almost collided with Jane, still intent on his postcard. She spoke his name just in time. He looked up then, his face pale. His eyes swiveled from her to Jesse and back again. He looked maybe even more paranoid than he'd been the morning of the murder. Yesterday morning. It seemed so long ago.

"They're after me. I knew it." He thrust the postcard into Jane's hands.

She automatically moved the card closer to Jesse so that they could study it together. A black deckle edge surrounded a depiction of old-time convicts linked in a line held together at their ankles by a black chain. They wore prison garb of thick black and white stripes. The first guy stood on a piece of raw lumber. It looked like he was being fitted by a tailor. His posture was casual, and he sported a snappy Borsellino hat. The guy behind him wore a beret, his hands fisted at each hip, blank eyes staring straight into the camera. The six or seven guys behind the front men gradually faded into shadow. A caption across the top read *Having a great time, wish YOU were here*.

Jane looked at Jesse, who nodded. She flipped the postcard over. A small box of print at the top right corner had a title: Chain Gang. This shot down her idea that the convicts were being fitted by a tailor. Instead, the tiny box of information said they had been fitted with chains and walked in lockstep to factories around and inside the prison, taking turns carrying the sixteen-pound ball affixed to the chain.

This time she didn't look at Jesse before flipping the card back over. The ball was not evident. Maybe it was lurking in the shadows or had yet to be attached. Jesse had produced a small plastic bag, opened it, and held it out to her. She dropped the postcard, which had no further message but did include George's address, plus a postmark from Jackson, Michigan. Jackson Prison. Jacktown. The loudest, dirtiest, smelliest prison in all of Michigan. The smell, Jane recalled from some long-ago newspaper expose, came from a cockroach infestation.

The roaches in Florida were smaller than the

Michigan variety. Everyone called them palmetto bugs and didn't make a big deal if one was found dead in the kitchen. Jane shuddered. A roach was a roach.

George pinned his eyes on Jesse. "You're the detective dude! See, I told you guys. They're after me. They framed me for this murder." He looked petrified, and Jane couldn't blame him. The postcard was creepy.

"Why don't you call Barb?" She reached out and squeezed George's hand, trying to comfort the distressed former criminal. She never imagined she'd find herself here, friends with cops and crooks and being consulted on an actual police case. If Stan could see her now. But thoughts of Stan were fleeting. He'd been a big part of her life, a painful part, but now that he was gone, she hoped his soul was at rest. She simply didn't want to spend any more of her precious life thinking about him. Was that so wrong? Would Marisol love her more if she made what had been absent for so long present again? Jane doubted it.

"Good idea," George said. "Maybe I should keep that postcard so I can show it to Barb. Or take a picture."

"I've been in touch with Agent Stone." This information surprised both Jane and George. "She's waiting to hear from you."

George didn't question the detective. He nodded once at Jane and continued walking down to his place, pulling his phone out of his pocket before he even got inside the condo.

"Wow," Jane said. "Is he going to be okay?"

"He'll have the FBI looking out for him. And I've got your back. You have nothing to worry about."

Jane nodded, grateful for the video cameras she'd

once considered intrusive. Had there been a video of whoever had put the shirt in George's car? She didn't bother to ask need-to-know Jesse Singer.

"I'll need to take your prints at the station," he said, holding up the postcard in the clear plastic evidence bag.

"Oh. Right. Sorry."

"Not a problem. You want to drive yourself?"

"Of course." She was tired and hungry. Even the thought of spending more time with the detective couldn't raise her energy level. "I'm going to stop for a coffee on the way."

"Good idea," Jesse said. "I'll treat. Coffee at the PD is lousy."

She took her own car anyway, and they met at the coffee shop on the corner of Central Avenue by the police station, right across from the old Detroit Hotel, which was now a liquor store at ground level. The rest of the hotel had been converted into condos.

They got their drinks and sat outside, watching the people flow.

Jane snapped a photo of the hotel's fancy grill work spelling out *Detroit*.

"Funny story about that place," Jesse said. "Not sure it's true." He took a long sip of his coffee and set it down. "Rumor has it the town founders were partners. One was Russian, and one was from Detroit. They flipped a coin to see who got to name the town, and the Russian won. The guy from Detroit got to name a hotel after his birth city."

Jane shook her head and smiled. Maybe this was turning into a date after all.

****

At the police station, Jane changed her mind about the date idea when Jesse immediately handed her off to Officer Riley with a hasty "See ya."

Officer Riley didn't meet her eyes and was all business. No way was Jane calling her Patrice.

"Sign this," Riley said, sliding a one-page document across her desk.

Jane stood reading it. The release form for recordings at Waylon's. Fine.

"Follow me," Riley said, and Jane obeyed.

She got her fingers inky in a small white room the size of a closet.

They didn't talk, but once the work was done, Riley broke the ice. "Where'd you come up with that idea to paint a mermaid on your wall?"

"I didn't paint it. No talent in that area." Jane told her about the artist in Largo she'd found through a restoration furniture store that had a sideline in mermaid stuff.

"Yeah. Mermaids are big here," Riley said. "So, why the fingerprints?"

"I touched something that turned out to be evidence. Maybe."

Riley's expression was as avid as when she'd checked out Jane's décor. Jane wondered why Jesse hadn't told Riley about the postcard. He'd handed off his other duties to her, why not that, too? Would it be okay for Jane to tell her about FBI Barb? Maybe if they weren't at the police station. Jane's stomach growled. It was past dinner time, and the latte Jesse had bought her was just not holding off the hunger pangs.

"Sorry," Jane said.

"You need food," Riley noted.

Jane nodded.

"He never stops to eat. Keeps a stash of granola bars in his desk drawer." Jane knew Riley was talking about Jesse. "I'm off now. Want to grab some dinner?"

"Okay," Jane said. "I've got my car."

"Do you know Brownie's on Gulf Boulevard? They have excellent burgers. And steak." She stood for a second before adding, "Also wine."

"Yeah. Madeira Beach, right?" They were on 1st Avenue, so a bit of a hike. Jane started plotting the route in her head. She could take the freeway or cut across 5th to Tyrone.

"Yep. I live there. Not on the beach, but in the city. My husband's on kid patrol. They already ate." Now the restaurant choice made sense. Okay, even more practical.

"Meet you there?" Jane figured she could think of Riley as Patrice now that they had a dinner date.

"Great." Patrice pointed Jane toward the exit just outside the area where her desk sat with several others, some occupied by uniformed cops. Jane had never socialized with a person in a police uniform. She wondered if Patrice would leave her shiny badge pinned to her blue shirt. Badges were badass.

Chapter Five

When Patrice showed up at Brownie's on the Beach (it was technically across the street from the Gulf), she was not wearing her uniform, thus no shiny badge. Jane was okay with that. She still felt safe as she waved Patrice over to the booth she'd scored.

"I would have ordered you a drink, but I wasn't sure what you liked," Jane said as Patrice sat down. Jane had already sipped from her martini. She'd have water with her meal just to be on best behavior.

"I'll have what she's having," Patrice told the waiter.

Jane smiled.

"Jesse told me about the postcard," Patrice said.

"Yeah, I don't know about that whole mob hit idea. I mean, why would the Detroit mob kill a Florida artist just to frame George? Seems like a lot of trouble. Why not just shoot George?"

Patrice nodded and practically grabbed her drink from the waiter's tray. She drank half the vodka in one sip and smacked her lips.

"Umm mmm," Patrice said, placing her drink on the table. "Long day."

"I bet. I looked up the stats, and you guys have way less crime than Detroit. Way fewer murders, especially." Detroit had about a murder a day. St. Pete was barely in the double digits. The cops had to be scrambling to catch that killer before the trail went cold.

"And people talk about southerners being gun crazy."

Patrice had a point.

"So what's George's story?"

Jane glanced at Patrice's ring finger. Nice band of gold but no diamond. Patrice was married, not dead, and George was super handsome. Like, movie star handsome.

Jane told Patrice about the charming ex-criminal who fell in love with an FBI agent after she'd arrested him at the mall.

"Whew," Patrice said, fanning her face with her menu. "I think I saw that movie."

Jane nodded, thinking of George's perfect white teeth and how the corners of his eyes crinkled when he smiled. It made him even more handsome. FBI Barb was a lucky lady.

"What about Jesse? Ah, Detective Singer?"

Patrice laughed. "What do you want to know?" She gestured to her faded T-shirt. "He dresses way better than me."

Jane thought back to Jesse's black silk shirt this morning. The black slacks that fell so neatly down to his leather shoes. He dressed better than her, too.

"He's a fashion plate," Jane said. "But he still got dirty with me today." Shoot. She hadn't meant it that way. Patrice just laughed when Jane blushed. "Should I call you Patrice or what?"

"Patrice is cool. My friends call me Patti. I can't get anybody to call me Patrice. I like it better. We could be friends...let's say you've got a potential new friend," Patrice clarified.

"That's nice. You seem only a little older than my daughter. I've got more potential with you than I do with her at present." Jane winced and changed the subject. "So what's the story with you and Jesse? Why doesn't he have a partner?"

"He does. His partner's on vacation. Key West. You know you can take the jet boat there. It's only about four hours."

Jane liked looking at big water, but her feet preferred dry land.

"I'm filling in. I'm up for a promotion in six months. I need to do something to distinguish myself. Like solve this murder. So you sure it isn't the Detroit mob?"

Jane shook her head. "It doesn't make sense. But maybe I read too many mysteries."

"You civilians!" Patrice said.

They both polished off their drinks.

"Who could it be?" Patrice lowered her voice and leaned in. "What do you think about the neighbors? Would someone kill Waylon because his yard was unusual?"

Jane thought about Pip. "There is one guy who was pretty hostile." The waiter asked if they wanted another round. They declined and gave their food orders. When he left, Jane recalled her interaction with Pip. "He spit on the ground and called me a white woman."

"Well, but you are." Patrice had subtle Asian features, nothing Jane had noticed before this minute.

"I know. It was the way he said it. And the spitting."

"Yeah," Patrice said.

"Kim, you know my friend, the one who was

dating Waylon, she told me Pip is a lamebrain. And Waylon didn't like him. The feeling was mutual."

"Really?" Patrice widened her eyes.

"Yep. Pip likes Mary, Waylon's friend. He's short, you know, so he seems to have some kind of grudge against the world."

"I'm short," Patrice said.

"You are. But with women it's different."

Patrice nodded. "We didn't find probable cause for Pip."

"I would think his bad attitude was cause enough."

"Nope. Fourth amendment. Now maybe I could work on his spitting at you as a misdemeanor, but since I didn't see it, I'd need a warrant. And it's too petty to go through the paperwork."

"Another cop saw. Maybe." Jane wasn't sure who witnessed Pip spit at her except Kim. Possibly George.

"Would you press charges?" Patrice asked.

"Probably not."

"There you go. Anyway, I need something tangible."

"You can't just search every house on the block?" Jane asked.

"No, ma'am."

"Let me guess. Fourth Amendment."

"Quick learner," Patrice said.

Jane and Patrice ate their dinner. They split the check; they'd both had a martini and a burger. When the waiter walked away with their credit cards, Patrice went back to Pip. "He could be the guy. Hotheaded. Loses his cool over a woman. Speaking of…" Patrice let her sentence dangle.

"What?" Jane said.

"You and Singer?"

"Yeah. What?"

The waiter brought their credit card slips.

"He likes you."

"I like him too," Jane admitted.

"But he's…well let's just say he's not known for his romantic ways."

Jane wasn't sure what that meant. "You mean he doesn't date much?"

"Not at all, is what I'm saying." Patrice scooted across the booth and stood.

"That's fine," Jane said, getting up. Jesse sounded like another workaholic. She'd learned her lesson with Stan. What she wanted was to dive into the new Lee Child novel she'd uploaded on her Kindle last night. But then she remembered she was trying to break her mystery reading habit. At least it wasn't a British mystery. Child was a Brit, but he wrote like an American. His character was an American.

"I think Singer might make an exception for you. I'd bet on it. But he'll be all work and no play until this murder is solved. That's just the job."

"Really?" An exception from his empty love life for her? "I can't tell." Jane was already past her one-minute crush. Another somebody who worked all day and night? No. Thank. You.

They walked out to the parking lot. On the patio, a guy played guitar. David Bowie. "The Man Who Sold the World." Jane thought of Kurt Cobain singing that on MTV Unplugged and how she'd taped it and watched it over and over again when she was young. Her parents had not minded. David Bowie was their world and Kurt hers. That song still got to her, even now, right here. Music had to be the most powerful thing on earth. Like love, if you find it.

"Yeah, he's got that elusive thing going on. Even with me. He should have brought me with him today, but he slipped away before I could tag along. Then I found out he was with you at the victim's residence and decided not to bother you guys."

"I was disappointed not to see the studio." Jesse Singer could work himself to death for all she cared. No, not death. A life of continued emptiness. Maybe it was different for men. Maybe they didn't get lonely. Maybe they didn't need love. But then she thought of Danny and how much he loved Julie. Some men needed love *and* work in their lives. Those were the best sort of men, in Jane's opinion. A balanced life was a happy life. Jesse didn't seem sad, but then neither had Stan. Just distracted.

"I kind of got that from the transcript I typed for him while you two sipped coffee together at the cafe." Patrice's response cut into Jane's thoughts. "You wanted to see his studio because you were wondering if Waylon made his own beads? Like if there was glass-blowing equipment?"

Jane nodded. It wouldn't prove who murdered Waylon. Purely academic interest.

Patrice nodded back.

Jane caught her expression under a parking lot light. "This is me," Patrice said, pointing to a red SUV.

"So he did? Blow his own glass?"

Patrice nodded again. She smiled as she swung open her car door. "See ya, Jane."

"Bye, Patrice." Huh. Cops in books never gave hints about homicides to civilians.

****

Jane got home just in time to see Kim heading over to the line dancing class at the clubhouse.

"Come on, Jane," Kim insisted. "It's good for you."

Jane had had a long day, and she'd wanted to go to yoga in the morning. But also, she wanted to be supportive of Kim right now. And she wanted to learn to line dance. So she went with Kim where she grapevined left as all the other widows went right. After class, they walked home. The cool down, Kim called it, even though they cooled down with a solo waltz in class. Jane loved how they waved their arms through the air so gracefully. Well, she attempted grace. The teacher and Kim embodied it.

"So, did I tell you about the video?" Kim asked.

"No," Jane said. She was tired. And she needed another shower. That was one of the million different things about Florida. Two showers a day was not that unusual. Even in November.

"They don't have video of the parking lot," Kim said. "We're supposed to have that camera working, but they never fixed it after Irma blew it to bits in 2017."

Jane's parents had been visiting her in Detroit in 2017. They'd missed Hurricane Irma, which had caused some major headaches in St. Pete, but no loss of life. Mostly power outages and uprooted trees. Now Irma had belatedly ripped away an important clue in the murder of Waylon Silvercloud. Or the condo association had done it by neglect.

"Why doesn't George park in the garage anyway?" Kim said.

"The homeowners use it for their personal stuff. I

think George said they've got a car in there. He doesn't have a key or anything."

"They'd have the guy who killed Waylon if only the parking lot camera had been working," Kim said, sounding sad.

"Maybe. Do they even know if the blood on the shirt was Waylon's?"

"Oh, honey. It was. You know how he liked those old checked flannel shirts with the arms cut off?"

Jane nodded. "Yeah. The few times I saw him when driving by, he was wearing one."

"Well, that detective, Singer, he took me down there to the car before they took it away with them. He had me look at the shirt through the window. It was Waylon's shirt. And his blood, too. I'm glad George didn't do it. He doesn't have a garage key, so there's no way he could have gotten out of his condo without being recorded by the walkway camera."

Jane wasn't sure how Kim had identified Waylon's blood, but she wasn't going to remark on it. Kim's voice edged on tears, and Jane didn't want to tip her over. "Wait. How could anyone go from their condo to the garage elevator without being seen?"

They were in front of their building now. Kim stopped at the steps. "You're right. I'm just tired," she said. "Only the first floor could do that. Because we have front doors and back doors."

Jane knew they were standing in the back of the building, but since that's where most of the four floors had their only outside door, she called it the front. The true front of the building had a vast slash of green lawn and an ornate park bench set before an American flag, often flown at half-mast for owners who had passed away. Jane saw this true front through her sunroom windows, and beyond it the boulevard lined with palms and the road to the clubhouse and gate.

Kim had a "real" front door that opened into her sunroom. Everyone on the first floor did. How nice for them.

"There's no camera on the front doors," Kim said. "So if George had been on the first floor, he could have just walked out his front door and down the sidewalk without a camera seeing him. Then he'd go through his garage out to the parking lot."

Jane wondered now if the two doors were a safety concern.

"George wouldn't know that the condo association hadn't fixed the parking lot camera after Irma. I didn't know," Jane said.

"The only one who would know that would be…well, I guess most of us knew the camera was broken. Nobody said anything. We didn't want a dues hike."

"What was that handyman's name again?"

"Fred?" Kim said it like a question, like how could anyone who lived here not know the handyman's name. Kim not only knew everybody's name, but she never forgot a face. She had the sharpest memory in the community.

"That's it. So did you hear about the broken camera from Fred?"

"Oh my stars. I do not know," Kim said. She laughed, Jane was happy to note. Kim had been knocked flat by Waylon's death. But she was strong, and she'd picked herself up and danced tonight. "That was at least three hurricane scares ago!"

Jane thought about the lack of parking lot cameras as she walked up the steps to her place, trying to pin down some elusive thought before dropping it. The night was full of sound. Insects, owls, a television blaring FOX News from Unit 200. Mr. Ansten couldn't hear and wouldn't wear hearing aids. He still had his storm door open to the screen, which had been everybody's habit except Jane's until the murder. Kim said it was like a code, if your door was open, anybody was welcome to walk right in.

Jane knew Beth, Mrs. Ansten, from yoga. Beth said she wore noise-cancelling headphones every time the television came on. Jane put the key in her lock, thinking about what Kim had said. Something nagged her, like a puzzle piece that didn't quite fit. What was it? She came into her long hallway, hung up her key on the driftwood-shelf hook shaped like a starfish, then locked and dead-bolted the door, and waited out the five seconds it usually took for short-term memory to kick in.

Oh. Yes. Probable cause. Would the police have had "probable cause" to suspect condo owners on the first floor of their building? Could the killer be living in her building? On the first floor? Or could it be Fred? Did Jesse know about the busted camera? He had to, and he had to have figured out that the first-floor owners would have had access to George's car. But it was weird. Why bring a bloody shirt home with you if you don't want anyone to know you'd just murdered somebody?

Her phone was ringing. George.

"Hey, George."

"Get the bourbon out."

"So nice of you to ask. I'm fine. How are you?"

"Would I be begging for bourbon if I was fine?"

He had a point. She opened the cupboard and grabbed bourbon and a glass. By the time she remembered he didn't use ice, he was walking through to the sunroom. He grabbed the cut crystal glass like it was a plastic cup and swigged down the liquor as he took his seat. His cloudy eyes projected his misery.

"Did you call Barb?"

"Yep." He finished the glass off in two swallows and put it on the table. Jane poured another one, but he didn't pick it up. "She said she was ready to reactivate my CI status." He spit the words like they were poison and hoisted the glass to his open mouth again.

Poor George. Not that she knew what he was talking about, but it didn't seem like a good thing.

"Listen, George, don't fall for a cop. Especially FBI. They're all workaholics. They have odd hours and unpredictable schedules."

"Oh, don't worry. We're not involved." He wiped his forehead with the arm attached to the hand that held the glass of bourbon. No chance of a spill, he'd sucked it down to an inch. "There's a rule. No personal relationship with a CI. No friendship, no socializing, and certainly no sex."

"Are you in love or just hot for her?"

"I love her, Jane. I told you that the day I met you."

"So what is a CI, and why do you have to be one?"

"Confidential informant. She's updating her file on the Detroit mob, and the postcard is part of it."

"Well, she's in Detroit and you're here, so not much of a chance for romance anyway."

Jane got up to make herself a martini. Misery loves

company. "You hungry?"

"Nah," George said.

They raised the volume of their words due to the shaking of the vodka and ice. Jane's cocktail shaker was covered in fake alligator skin. It was only big enough to make one perfectly chilled martini. She poured her drink, skipping the olives, and went back out to sit across from George. Then she got up and shut her blinds and turned on a few lights.

"Did you lock the door when you came in?"

"What? No."

She went down the hall to take care of that.

"You're paranoid."

"Nope. Listen." And then she told him about the broken camera in the parking lot and how anybody who lived on the first floor could be the murderer who put the bloody shirt in George's car. Then she sipped her martini.

"Huh," George said. "Does Singer know?"

"I assume he does." Jane didn't want to think about Jesse Singer.

"I thought you two were collaborating?"

"Oh, no. That was a one-shot deal. He needed me to assess the art, but I didn't find any clues to who killed Waylon or anything like that."

"I'm telling you, Jane, law enforcement, they're all the same. They'll use you and spit you out."

Jane didn't think that was true. Patrice wasn't using her, for example. "I think they just work all the time. Their job is their life. Jesse was married. Divorced! I read that between 50 percent and 75 percent of married law enforcement eventually get a divorce. It's the job. Don't borrow trouble."

They brooded over their alcohol like jilted lovers do. Not that either of them had made it quite to lover status.

"You know, she kissed me once." George finished off his third bourbon and went to the kitchen to fill his glass with water. He came back, ready to tell Jane the story. Not for the first time, either.

"You did tell me that, George. She may really like you, but she just likes her job better." Jane didn't mention that he was a former criminal, but that was probably a big part of why Barb didn't want to have any kind of personal relationship with George.

"FBI Barb. She'll be mad if she hears me call her that."

Jane wasn't sure how Barb would hear that dubious term of endearment since she was several states up I-75. "Wait. Is she coming here?" Jane remembered how Singer had known something about Barb. He'd been in contact with her. He probably had already sent the postcard to her via special government courier or something. And he'd said Barb had George's back. Jane reminded George of Jesse's words. "Maybe she's coming here. Maybe there have been further developments in the case you worked on. Maybe that's why she wants to reactivate your status as a co-worker."

"CI," George said. "It's not like you and the detective."

"That's done. It was a one-off."

"But you like him."

"Ha. I don't. He works too much, which makes him disconnected, which makes him unable to form attachments, which makes him distant, which is exactly what my husband was, and I do not want that again."

George tipped his head to one side and stared at her. "Okay," he said.

Chapter Six

Special Agent Barbara Stone arrived at the Detroit field office early on the morning of November 12. She had a bad feeling about that postcard sent to George Sanders from Jackson State Prison. She'd been reading through her files on the case, trying to find probable cause to question the prisoners.

Only three of the less important members of the Detroit mob landed in Jackson. The others were in Super Max. She simply wanted permission to drive down to Jacktown and question three criminals. They'd called themselves the Detroit mob, but they were babies. Babies without consciences. Babies who had been playing in bad sandboxes.

A bulletin pinged on her phone. Before she could read it, Duffy, Special Agent in Charge, texted her. *Meeting NOW.* Had to be about the alert, meaning it had something to do with one of her cases. She checked her phone as she grabbed up her files.

One Louie Donaldsin had just walked off the prison farm in Jackson. Louie Donaldsin was the low man on the Detroit mob ladder. He'd gotten several charges dropped and was doing easy time compared to his fellow mobsters. She peeked at the file she'd scooped up as she walked down the hall to the meeting. Her squad supervisor would be there. This was probable cause. Louie'd been up for parole in five years. It made no sense he'd skip, but then criminals weren't known for being sensible people. Still she didn't get it. What's not to like about picking vegetables in the fresh air? She located Louie in her notes and read quickly through the index on him.

She passed Ona, her favorite clerk, and requested the squad be sent digital copies of the Detroit mob report. Barb was proud of the work she'd done on that case. She'd gone undercover and flipped a suspect, earning respect from her mostly male peers and superiors. She'd deserved it, but it had cost her more than she liked to admit.

"Close the door," Duffy said. She clocked five agents in the room. Every one of them outranked her. "You contact your CI?"

"Yes. He's resisting reactivation." She left out the part about how George missed her and didn't she miss him even a little and how he wasn't wrong, he knew they'd had a connection. And that kiss. She especially was not going to think about that lapse in judgement. "He's lying low in Florida."

Everyone was looking at their pinging phones. Ona, bless her.

"I sent you all the final report," Barb said. "Louie Donaldsin has a mother in Clearwater. We have a current address. Clearwater is three towns north of St. Petersburg, where my CI has established residence and also where the postcard was sent by someone from the Jackson."

Duffy nodded, then said, "We have Jackson and the track down I-75 covered. I'm sending you to Florida. You've set up contact with the local PD, correct?"

"Yes," Barb replied, no notes needed. "Homicide Detective Jesse Singer. A current murder case of his involves George Sanders, my CI on the Detroit mob case, in a peripheral way." Duffy knew this, but had he read the others in?

Duffy finished her brief. "Someone planted a bloody shirt belonging to a local murder victim in Sanders's rental car. Sanders was cleared, but he received an unsigned postcard from Jackson. Detective Singer was onsite working the case, and Sanders showed him the card."

Barb closed her file and opened her phone. "I'm sending you my preliminary report on that case." She forwarded the digital file as she spoke. "At this time, we do not believe the cases are connected."

She organized each detail of what she needed to do next in her head and laid out what the guys needed to know. "I'll meet with the fugitive's mother as soon as I arrive. He has no other living relatives, and all his known friends and associates are in jail. I'll alert Sanders in the event Donaldsin decides to make contact." Nobody said what they all were thinking. If Donaldsin contacted Sanders, it might be with a bullet. "I'll call Detective Singer on the way to the airport. He can put someone on Sanders and smooth the way with local law enforcement, arrange for Donaldsin's photo to land with Seminole County Sheriff and Clearwater PD."

Everyone nodded. Their nods meant two things: they had confidence in her and they were focusing on the big picture.

"Your plane leaves in two hours," Duffy said. "Ona's sending your boarding pass, and she'll file the paperwork for your weapon. You'd best be on the road."

****

Barb introduced herself to the pilot and asked an attendant about other law enforcement onboard. This was a courtesy and also a way to avert confusion in the unlikely event of an incident during the flight. Nope, she was the only person carrying a concealed weapon aboard the flight to Tampa. She settled in her seat having assessed the other passengers and noting no potential problems. She casually surveyed the progress of the drinks cart, not for herself, agents didn't drink when they carried firearms on planes, not even if they were on vacation, which she was not. Much as she'd love a glass of wine, she was working 24-7 until she captured Donaldsin. So instead of ordering a cocktail, she familiarized herself with who might be ordering three vodkas at a time. Since it was a morning flight, only one woman, approximately fifty years old, clearly an anxious flier, was double drinking. Her husband was with her, patting her arm as she swigged, so Barb relaxed.

She'd done everything she could do until she landed in Tampa. She allowed her mind to roam. It predictably landed on George. He'd had been pleased when she'd phoned him en route to Metro. She hadn't told him Donaldsin had escaped. She would do that in person. He'd offered to pick her up in Tampa. She said no. She didn't tell him she'd be checking in with the field office downtown, where a vehicle waited for her. She'd already touched base with the satellite office in Pinellas County, too.

Resident agents in the field office had sweet

postings, the dream job Barb wanted. She had long ago put her name on the list, which went by seniority. She had twelve years on the job, had done good work. She deserved this move. It wasn't exactly a promotion, more lateral. It just depended on who was ahead of her on the list. When a job came up, wherever it was, she'd take it. She'd move anywhere. RAs were rural, away from the big city field offices, thus they had better hours and lighter caseloads. As an RA, she could start a family. She was thirty-five. If she waited until the usual twenty-year retirement, she'd be well into her forties. They had a name for that. Geriatric pregnancy. In fact, she was technically already there.

Most of the guys had families. They also had wives who picked up the slack. Kids who loved them and respected their jobs. Duffy had gone to his kids' school to talk about his career in the Bureau. He'd asked her to accompany him, so girls would be inspired, too. She went, which didn't help her baby fever. Forget it, she told herself. She'd done what she could, now she had to take the next steps in order. Until she got RA, she wouldn't marry or start a family. That had been her five-year plan, seven years ago. She'd never get a wife; she wasn't wired that way. She'd be getting a husband. And they were a different species.

George had reminded her that he was still refusing to sign the CI agreement. That was fine. She didn't need him for that. She quickly cut off any thought of why she really needed him by opening her laptop and adding to her ongoing report. She deplaned without incident and within an hour was at the rehab facility where Dorothy Donaldsin was recovering from gall bladder surgery.

A morphine drip IV plugged into Dorothy, but she opened her eyes, alert when Barb said hi at the door.

"Hi, there," Dorothy said. "Come on in. What will I be signing this time?" Okay, good. Coherent, too.

"Nothing to sign." Barb flashed her badge and introduced herself.

"Let me see that badge again," Dorothy said.

Barb obliged, keeping it just out of reach.

"So, I always wondered. Does that shield stay on with Velcro? Or is it pinned?"

"The former."

"Ah." Dorothy nodded. "You must be here about my son."

"Have you talked to Louie lately?"

"Of course. He's coming down to see me. It's not easy having surgery when you're eighty years old."

"Oh. Well, that's good. I mean, not that your surgery was difficult. I hope you heal quickly from that. But it's good Louie's coming to see you."

"He got special permission from the prison."

Barb nodded. "Did he say what day he'd be here?"

"No. Just that he'd be here no matter what."

Barb slid her card across the table tray.

Dorothy looked at it, then after a slight hesitation, picked it up and examined it. "He didn't do anything wrong, did he?"

People didn't give octogenarians enough credit. Dorothy was sharp as a tack.

"I'd like to speak to him." Barb avoided answering Dorothy's question, and she was sure the white-haired woman realized it.

"He's a good boy, really."

"With you for a mom, I bet he is." Barb was not a

gambler, but Dorothy didn't have to know that. She wondered if that was all this was. Louie had escaped to visit his mother after surgery. Had he asked for leave and been denied?

Chapter Seven

"She's coming," George yelled into Jane's intercom.

Jane was cleaning house, which took far less time than had her larger family home in Detroit. She dropped her duster on the end table and rushed down the hall, past her mermaid, and to the door. Despite how little work it was keeping a home for one, Jane loved any excuse to postpone cleaning.

"Wow!" Jane said. "Wish I had champagne!" Florida was basically one party after another. She'd cracked more than one bottle of Brut since she'd been here.

"I'm thinking I should have a ring. How can she say no if I go down on one knee and ask?" George stood at the mermaid's tail, holding up the wall.

"You wanna come in?"

"Naw, just wanted to share the news." They didn't need champagne; George was bubbling away without it.

Jane felt bad for George. Young people didn't get it. Love wasn't fate or soul mates, it was just hormones that evaporated with time. But he looked so hopeful.

"So the job is paying well?" Jane said.

George worked as a mechanic at the auto shop on Tyrone.

"It's not bad. But I can make payments on a ring, am I right?"

Jane didn't think George's credit would be very good, what with him being a former criminal and all, but she hated to burst his bubble. "You know what kind of ring she'd like?" Jane asked. She'd longed for gold, but Stan had insisted on silver. The one he chose reminded her of a beer tab, but she'd been so disappointed about the band of gold from her dreams slipping away that she hadn't said anything. Maybe she should give her ring to George. Was that bad luck?

"No. Can't say I do. I've never wanted a wife before."

Jane wanted to give her ring to George. He could trade it in or something. But she should save it for Marisol. She had Stan's ring too, for Danny. The kids didn't know, but she'd asked the undertaker to slip Stan's ring off after the viewing and before they closed the casket. The guy had given it to Jane in a tiny manila envelope marked with Stan's name. She kept it filed with her papers and her own ring in the little fireproof safe she'd brought from Detroit. She didn't think of Detroit as home anymore. None of her family was there. Friends, yes, but none of them were widows yet. Somehow being among widows comforted her.

She was daydreaming. George. Advice. Stat.

"First you should take her to the Tyrone Mall. Just browse the shops. There's got to be a jewelry store."

"Oh, there is."

Oops. George had already cased the mall.

"I can't help it," he said, a slight blush rising over his tan. "Just a habit."

"I know. You're a good guy."

"I am. I'm not like a rat or whatever. I took that job with the Detroit mob because I thought it was good acting practice. Everyone says how handsome I am, so I thought, well, if I can do that, maybe I'll go to Hollywood. It was stupid. I know that now. I met Barb, a one in a million woman, and she wants nothing to do with me. She thinks I'm bent, but I'm not."

"You are handsome, George." Did he really not know that?

"Yeah, that's what people say, but it does me zero good. Barb has frozen me out. But maybe—I mean, she's here. That's got to mean something. Maybe we can meet up at the mall. She texted she wants to see me tonight. She said somewhere public."

"Okay, the mall is perfect. So what you do is you ease her over to the jewelry store and ask what kind of ring she likes."

"Isn't that a little obvious?"

"Maybe, but if she's anything like me, she'll appreciate you asking her opinion."

"Women are a mystery, that is for sure. But hell, okay, I'll do it."

The opening riff to Metallica's "Enter Sandman" interrupted their conversation. George looked at his phone. "It's her," he said. "I gotta go." He was out the door so fast Jane didn't get to say goodbye.

****

The next morning, Jane was running late for yoga class. As she locked her door, George came out of nowhere, racewalking by with an ugly plant and hardly a glance.

"Well, hello to you, too, neighbor." Then she looked down the row of condo units where George had come from. With a beaded plant. What? A mini Waylon? "What's that?" She had to speed after him.

87

"Nothing. I can't talk now." George burst through his door. He left it open. Code for come in.

Jane looked down the row of units. Next to her, unit 203 had been empty since Carl, her sweet neighbor she'd only known for a few weeks, had died. Unit 204 was Cat Lady, a nice woman, kept to herself, except when she took her cats out for walks on the leashes the association insisted on. Unit 205 was the large corner unit. Kim said a doctor had bought it as an investment. Everybody knew that he had weekly revolving renters in March and April. Strictly against association rules, more Airbnb than Winding Bayou. Nobody knew how he got away with it. For now, the unit was empty, so who had given George that fake Waylon? Surely not the Cat Lady?

Jane opened George's screen and entered his empty hallway. She made it to the living room in time to see him stashing the plant on top of a bookshelf.

"George!" She pulled her phone out of her pocket and lined up a photo of the plant to send to Patrice. George blocked the shot, putting a hand over her phone screen. "What are you doing? That could be evidence."

"Evidence? Of what?"

"Waylon's beads are on that ugly plant!" Jane couldn't take her eyes off the monstrosity. The beads were Waylon's colors, and some of them gave off a similar luster, but they weren't stringed. Gobs of clear glue held each bead in place on the spindly fake plant leaves. She tried to edge in closer but stopped when she heard a radio-like static coming from the plant. "What the…"

George grabbed her arms and raised a finger to his lips in the classic *shhh* pose.

"George, you there?" The plant was talking.

"Houston, we have a problem," George said.

Jane's eyes widened. "George, tell me right now what is going on!"

"Calm down, little lady," said a guy with the plant voice, suddenly appearing from the hall. Jane looked from George to the guy wearing snowbird attire head to toe, except for the gun hanging out of the waistband of his lime green shorts. The shirt sported more pink flamingoes than she'd seen in her entire time here in Florida, but they didn't camouflage the gun.

"Jane, this is Tom Benton. He's an agent from the FBI." Tom Benton flashed his badge. Jane was becoming immune to the allure of the shiny stars. "He's protecting me. One of those guys I put away escaped from Jackson, and they think he's heading here!"

"Whoa, cowboy," Tom Benton said.

George already looked calmer. "Jane's okay. She lives next door to you in 202," he said.

Since nobody was paying any particular attention to her, she edged closer to the horrid fake Waylon and snapped a photo. Before the FBI could confiscate her phone, she sent the photo to Patrice. "The local police will want to see that plant," Jane said.

"What? Why?" Tom Benson asked.

Jane told him.

He nodded, grabbed the plant, and pulled a tiny device out of it. "I'll find something else," he told George, walking out.

Her phone chimed. Jesse Singer. She remembered with regret how she'd once thrilled to see his name on her phone screen. She put him on speaker.

"Better come back, Special Agent Tom Benson,"

Jane said, instead of saying hello to Detective Singer. "I've got St. Pete PD on the line."

Benton hadn't made it all way down the hall. He came back.

"Sorry," he said toward the phone Jane was holding up. "My bad." And then he left.

"Jane. I see the FBI has read you in," Jesse said.

"If you mean, did I find a fake Waylon the FBI next door was using for audio surveillance in George's condo, you'd be correct," she said.

"Patrice is on her way," Jesse said. Then he hung up without saying goodbye. Fine. He was behaving exactly like her emotionally absent husband had when he'd been alive.

"So George." Jane sat on the uncomfortable and aesthetically awful wicker sofa. "What happened with Barb yesterday?"

He came out of the kitchen with two coffees, handing her one.

"I'm glad you know." He looked around as if to be sure they were not being listened in on. "About the agent living next door to you. I didn't like keeping it from you."

Jane let herself feel what she was feeling. Warm with friendship and surprised by excellent coffee. George had even poured her beverage into a mermaid mug from a tourist shop at John's Pass. Jane knew because she'd considered buying a set but then decided she liked her Franciscan Desert Rose cups just fine. They had been a wedding gift from her parents. She'd wrapped each piece, boxed it herself, and had it shipped to her folks' house. It was the only memento of her life in Detroit that she'd brought with her to Florida. Well, except those wedding rings.

"I still don't know what happened with Barb," Jane said. "Did you meet at the mall?"

"Yes." George sighed out the word. "I notice you're just calling her Barb now, no *FBI* involved."

"Probably wouldn't be cool, you know, if I met her. When you invite me to the wedding. Is there going to be a wedding?"

Not that there was anything wrong with the nickname FBI Barb. Or female FBI agents. In fact, they really should make an FBI doll. She could have a little gun for an accessory. And sneakers instead of impossibly high heels.

"Doubtful." George sighed like he was in drama class and had just been commanded to act despondent. "We met at the mall. Outside. For about two minutes. We didn't even get inside the mall. She told me about Louie—he's the guy who escaped, incredible! I didn't think he had the balls. No offense. Anyway, they have a dragnet, or whatever they call it, on Louie. Tom, the guy guarding me, works out of Tampa. I don't know why Barb isn't guarding me. She did last time. I mean, some of the time. I had three different agents who rotated sitting in cars while I watched bad cable in my hotel room."

"But only Barb kissed you."

"Yeah, well, the other two were guys. Not that there's anything wrong with men marrying each other. I'm all for that. It's just not my thing is all."

"It's probably better someone is here round the clock," Jane said.

"Yeah. They gave me a car." George did not sound happy that his car, currently evidence in a murder investigation, had been replaced by the FBI. "I liked the anonymous privacy of Uber. This one's got some kind of tracker on it."

"So," Jane asked, "are they're letting you work?"

"Yeah, well, just for a few hours here or there when they need me to be bait."

That sounded dangerous to Jane. George was more than bait. Barb didn't deserve him. But she was finished telling him that. He looked sad enough. He didn't even seem afraid, which would be anybody's natural reaction to being hunted by an escaped prisoner and former gang member from Detroit. There had to be more George wasn't telling her. "What else?"

"I signed the CI agreement."

That Confidential Informant thing he talked about before.

"I thought you weren't going to do that."

"I had to. They protect me; I help them. That's the way it works. But it also means I am Barb's rat and thus cannot be her boyfriend."

Jane liked the sound of Barb less and less. She was using George and crushing his spirit at the same time. Bitch Barb was more apt than FBI Barb. But George had it bad for her. He was doing this, being bait, for Barb. Jane was glad she had decided not to let Jesse get to her. Not that he was even trying, but still.

"Jane? You in there?" Patrice yelled through the screen door. Still open.

Good way to guard somebody, Tom Benton, Jane thought.

"Come on in, everybody else does," George said. To Jane he whispered, "Everyone but Barb, that is."

"You should lock your door."

"Naw. Benton'll be back. This is our last chance to have a conversation he doesn't hear."

"Who's Benton?" Patrice said, already clicking her digital recorder on.

"FBI," George and Jane said at the same time.

"Did I hear my name?" Benton was only a long hallway behind Patrice.

"Did you know the FBI was guarding George?" Jane whispered as Tom Benton appeared.

Patrice shook her head.

Jane was glad she'd sent Patrice the photo. Jesse was being a typical workaholic, feeling like he had to do everything himself or it wouldn't get done right. At least he'd sent Patrice here instead of showing up himself. Jane wanted this arrest of the fake plant man/possible murderer for Patrice. First they'd have to find him. She wondered if the fake plant was probable cause to search Pip's house.

After everyone was introduced, Patrice bagged the fake Waylon plant. Agent Tom gave George a cat figurine, showing him the mike on the back. Then he placed it where the fake plant had been. He explained to Patrice that he knew the story about Waylon and the bloody shirt and the murderer on the loose, which in Jane's mind was way more dangerous than an escaped convict.

When Patrice left, Jane followed her down the hall and walked her down to the cop car she'd parked in the lot. Jane wondered if the FBI had fixed the surveillance camera. She wished she'd asked Agent Tom Benton.

"What's up?" Patrice said.

"That fake plant. The beads are Waylon's, but the fake plant is not his work. Somebody stole those beads, probably from his work studio. Maybe it was a regular thing until Waylon came in and caught him at it, and that's why he was murdered."

"Whoa, sister, you've got quite the imagination."

Jane thought the dots connected pretty clearly. "Really? It doesn't make sense? I was hoping the plant would give you probable cause to search Pip's house."

"Well…" Patrice said. "Are you sure these beads are Waylon's?"

"As sure as I can be without comparing them to the glass in the studio."

"So…pretty sure, then?"

Jane nodded.

Patrice looked thoughtful. Thinking cop thoughts, most likely.

"Maybe I'll swing by Mary's and ask her if she's ever seen a plant like this for sale at the farmer's market."

"Flea market more like," Jane said. "The stuff at the farmer's market is much nicer."

Patrice nodded. "Thanks, Jane." She got in her squad car and pulled out of the parking lot.

Jane wondered if she should have shared her suspicions about Fred the handyman. But no. That would just make her seem paranoid, although paranoia in this case seemed like a normal type of response. She started back upstairs as women holding rolled yoga mats streamed from the clubhouse.

Damn, she'd missed yoga.

Chapter Eight

The next day, leaving coffee at the clubhouse with Kim, Jane screamed and threw her open purse to the ground.

Kim grabbed Jane's arm with one hand and clutched her heart with the other. "What's wrong?"

"There's a huge rat in my purse!"

Jane stood rigid as coffee group stragglers filed out of the clubhouse. Kim went over to the shrubbery and kicked Jane's purse with her toe. An iPhone and a fake braid fell out onto the tile. Kim grabbed the braid and shook it. "No rats here," she said.

Jane checked her phone. No cracks or chips on the screen. She took a photo of the braid Kim held up and texted it to her friendly police officer, Patrice. The phone worked just fine. Jane could hear the board meeting getting started in the clubhouse. Just another day at Winding Bayou. And possibly another clue.

"We should probably put that in a plastic bag," Jane said to Kim.

"By 'we' do you mean me?" Kim asked.

"I don't know where they keep things in the clubhouse kitchen," Jane said. Which was true.

Kim went back inside and came out with the braid bagged up just as Jane's phone chimed. Kim tucked the bagged braid in Jane's purse. Jane checked her phone. Jesse Singer. Jane took the call as she and Kim walked toward their building.

"Jane? What's with the braid? Is this related to Waylon? Because…"

"I know. Waylon didn't wear a braid. But the color of the hair and the symbolism…"

"Where are you?" Jesse said, cutting her off. So rude.

"Just leaving coffee hour in the clubhouse. Found the braid in my purse. There were a hundred people at coffee. Any one of them could have slipped that braid into my purse. But I think I know who did it."

Kim stopped to talk to a sweaty guy holding a tennis racket. Jane waved goodbye and kept walking.

"Why would someone do that?" Jesse asked.

"Remember? I told you. Wait, no I didn't." Her theory of the other day had seemed too thin almost as soon as she started thinking it.

"Take your time," Jesse said. To Jane his concern felt fake. "Start from the beginning."

Jane took a breath. "Okay, let me get inside my condo."

She sprinted up the stairs to her floor. She passed George's place. Locked up, shades drawn. The FBI agent who'd moved in on the other side of Jane was nowhere in sight, either. "I've got a new neighbor." She unlocked her door and went inside, flopping onto her sofa.

"Yes, I heard," Jesse said.

"Well, okay, so Kim was telling me that a video camera in the parking lot was knocked out during Irma a few years ago and has not been replaced. And then she said that the owners on the first floor don't have a camera outside the front doors down there. So whoever set up George for Waylon's murder could have been a Winding Bayou owner. One of us, well, someone on the first floor, could have planted that bloody shirt in George's car, and nobody would ever know."

"Yes," Jesse said. Jane swore she detected irritation in his tone. "What about the braid?"

"Well. When I was at coffee last week, before the murder, one of the people at my table—in fact, one of the owners of a first-floor condo in my building—said Waylon had a totem pole in his yard."

"Who?" Again with the rushing. And just after he'd told her to take her time. She wished Patrice didn't automatically pass all her clues on to Jesse, but it was probably a police rule.

"I don't know. I'll have to ask Kim his name. He's one of the married couples who sit with us for coffee. There are two married couples, plus Rich, Kim's admirer, and the rest of us widows. I don't know the married couples' names yet, but I know what this guy looks like. So Kim can tell me his name. He was at the dance last Saturday night before Waylon was killed. With his wife. The social committee posted dance photos on our website."

Jane got up and went across the sunroom to the wall of windows that looked down on a row of palm trees. Kim was still standing on the sidewalk talking to the guy with the tennis racket. "She's busy right now, but I'll text you his name."

"What about the braid?"

"I'm getting to that!" Jane took a breath. Her heart was hammering. She needed to light her peace candle. Or maybe she shouldn't have had that second cup of coffee. "Last week, at coffee, this guy with no name, he said Waylon had a totem pole in his yard. We both know there were zero totem poles in Waylon's yard. Today, I see same Mr. No Name at coffee again and find a braid in my purse."

Jane let the silence rest. She lit her peace candle. It smelled like cotton candy. Every art major understood semiotics, but as the silence continued, Jane wondered if cops knew that stuff.

"So." She decided to help Jesse out. "Both the totem pole and the braid are stereotypical symbols that signify Native American culture. The connotation in this context is an insult. Like sports teams naming themselves after Native American tribes. Or maybe the guy is just ignorant. Now that he's gone into my purse, it feels like he's sending me a message."

"I agree," Jesse said. "But why?"

"For some reason, maybe because I'm working with the police, I've been targeted by Mr. No Name. Maybe he wants to scare me. Maybe he killed Waylon. Maybe he really is worried about the price of his home being affected. Or maybe he's a racist. Or all of the above."

Just saying it out loud made her nervous. She paced from the sunroom to the living room and back again. Even her peace candle failed to calm her nerves. She checked her clock. Too early for wine. She went to the window again. Kim was gone, so was the guy with the tennis racket. Jesse was silent on the other end of the phone. Maybe he'd hung up in disgust. Just then, his words rode across the line.

"Is Kim available? Can you get her to ID your suspect? I'm coming over for that braid. Don't leave."

As usual, he didn't bother saying goodbye.

She called Kim. "Can you come up here?"

"Cops coming over?"

"Yes."

"On my way."

While she waited for Kim, Jane opened her laptop and found the email with the dance photos attached. She located Mr. No Name and his wife. She enlarged the photo. He looked like anybody else. That was the trouble with racists and murderers. Half the time they looked just like your neighbors.

When Kim got there, Jane showed her the photo.

"Oh, yeah, that's Natalie and Randy." She looked at Jane, her eyes slitted in thought. "Why? You think he put the braid in your purse?"

Jane explained her theory which was starting to feel like wet tissue paper. It just wasn't holding together. She liked Natalie. Even though she had a husband, a rare commodity here in Winding Bayou, she still got up and did all the line dances with the widows on Saturday night. Sure, Randy was an asshole, but that wasn't Natalie's fault.

"Hmm." Kim shrugged. "It's weird, I'll give you that. But Randy?"

"I know. Oh, and I didn't get to tell you at coffee. There's an FBI agent guarding George. He's moved in next door."

"Is he single?" Kim wondered.

"I don't know. He's about my son's age," Jane said. Danny was thirty.

Kim had left the door open, and Patrice shouted down the hall that they were coming in. Jane wondered about the fake Waylon plant she'd given Patrice yesterday. Did they know anything about that yet? And if they did, would Patrice tell her?

Jane made a point of avoiding Jesse's eyes and gave the braid to Patrice. "Jesse filled me in," Patrice said.

"She thought it was a rat," Kim said, chuckling.

"This the guy you think may have put the braid in your purse?" Patrice nodded at the laptop photo. Jane nodded. Kim spelled names and recited the address of Natalie and Randy.

Jesse told Patrice to take the braid down to the station for testing. Patrice left. Jesse told Kim she could go and remembered to thank her for her help. Now that they were alone, Jane still didn't want to look at Jesse, but her mother brought her up better than that. She powered down her laptop and turned away from the desk, meeting Jesse's eyes.

"What's happening with the fake Waylon plant?"

"I wanted to talk to you about that," Jesse said.

Jane wondered if she was finally going to be allowed into Waylon's work studio. He'd been killed in there, which was creepy, but she had a scholar's interest in the artist's tools. And she wanted to see Waylon's sheet glass and his canes. Canes were solid rounded cylinders made from sheet glass, less than a foot long. Jane was pretty sure Waylon made his own canes. The luster, quality, size, and color of the beads all pointed to something created originally, not mass produced. Waylon would have molds, torches for lamp work, and various other glass-working instruments. Maybe a furnace and a kiln. Depending where Waylon's glass had come from, she was pretty confident she'd be able to tell if the beads on the fake plant were indeed from Waylon's supply.

"Do you have time to go down to the shed?" Jesse asked.

"Of course." She didn't correct him when he said "shed" instead of work space or studio. It felt good to have her own expertise, and yes, it felt good that Jesse needed her help.

Jesse drove. Jane went with him. She could walk home after. The Seminole were still guarding the house and yard. The tent had been removed, and when they got out of the car and Jane got closer to Waylon's house, she saw that the installation had been partially deconstructed.

"Are you doing a recreation of the installation elsewhere?" Jane asked one of the Seminole cops.

"Yes," he said.

Jane wanted to ask him more questions, but Jesse took her arm and pulled her toward the back yard. "We'll be finishing up in the shed today," he said to the tribal guard.

"Excellent. I'll let the team know." The guard pulled a phone out of his pocket as Jesse unlocked the gate.

"So you said...so right now, this is it? You're handing everything off to the tribal police?"

"We're working the case together, but after you and I leave, they'll have Waylon's property back. There are plans in the works. Thanks to you, Waylon's art will live on."

Wow. Her work had paid off. People were giving Waylon his due. Too bad he had to die for it to happen.

Jesse gestured for Jane to follow him into the back yard. She walked toward the studio, noticing that Jesse waited for her to catch up. Okay, she'd give him points for manners. The back wall of the studio was brick and a chimney jutted out from the roof. It never got that cold in St. Pete. Unless you were blowing glass, then you needed big heat. Jesse handed Jane a pair of gloves, opened the lock with a key, and stepped aside so she could go in first.

"The crime lab has done extensive work in here," Jesse said, leaving the door open and turning on an overhead light. "Not much is how he had it. But we took photos so the Seminole Nation can replicate the working conditions more accurately. Everything has been tested and returned here for their ongoing project."

"And they're going to include his studio in the installation? Like, move it to a different location?"

"I hear they're discussing mounting the art pieces in a garden or a museum. I guess it's a garden outside the museum. And they're going to recreate the studio, too. I think they're sinking some cash into moving this building intact if they can get permissions. It's an impressive effort, Jane."

Jane knew the Seminole had several museums in the area. She'd been to a few of them with her mom. Now Waylon was being recognized with a permanent home for his work. Too bad they couldn't leave his installation and studio on the property, but there were probably zoning issues. Vandalism as well. Hadn't the fake plant bandit already ripped off some of Waylon's beads?

"Where'd you go, Jane?" Jesse said.

She snapped out of her musings and looked around. The first visual she studied were the sheets of glass, all primary colors, stacked in wooden crating next to the back wall. Then she looked over the items on the workbench, which was in the middle of the room. She put on her gloves, just in case. Glass canes in Waylon's unique lustrous colors—burnt orange, cloud vanilla, freshwater blue with darker sapphire wavy stripes all around the canes—nestled together in a wire basket, ready to become beads. She saw now exactly how Waylon had achieved that signature blue. Three torches of varying size lined one side of the desk. Flame work didn't require a fancy torch, but it looked like Waylon had upgraded a few times from basic to better.

"He'd need propane and oxygen," Jane said, looking around.

"Those items have not been returned here," Jesse said. "Too volatile."

Jane still didn't know how Waylon had been killed. She'd guessed he'd been stabbed with a point from one of the fence posts that surrounded his yard, but there was no wrought iron in the studio. Maybe the police still had it. Or could the killer have done something chemically that poisoned Waylon? She didn't bother asking. The police were not releasing those details, and they wouldn't until the murderer was arrested.

Jane glanced around the desk at graphite pads and rods, scoring knives, wire cutters, various pots and jars, special welding glasses. She guessed that one of the welding torches had been used to temper and burnish the copper shapes that had been planted amid the sawgrass out front. She went over to the sheet glass against the wall and bent at the knees to get a better look. The glass was of very best quality. That didn't surprise her.

"So, we're thinking he used the large sheets of glass to form the rods?" Canes were also called rods.

Jesse had done some research.

"Yes. It's a work-intensive process and likely why he has a furnace." Jane saw now that Waylon had needed the furnace and various torches for different steps in his process. "He blended colors of the sheet glass to get his unique coloration for the canes. Then the canes were fashioned into beads." She stood and walked over to the desk again. She took a cane and held it at both ends. Then she lowered it to a torch and carefully rotated the cane. She replaced the cane and picked up a wire cutter. "The cane gets hot and expands where the heat is applied. Once you have the size of bead you want, you quickly make a hole for stringing the beads, snip the round section from the cane, and cool it down."

"We analyzed the beads on the fake plant you found. They match Waylon's other beads." Jesse opened a drawer under the workbench surface. It had been divided into several cubicles; each held one color of the various finished beads. Altogether, Waylon had created twelve signature colors.

"There are a few more colors in here than what we saw during our examination of the original installation," Jane remarked, pointing to a mossy green group of beads. "These probably didn't show well with the flora."

"Yes. We noticed that."

"Perhaps he was still developing a few of these colors."

"Would he have given those beads to a friend? The less successfully colored ones?"

"It's possible. His family may have more information about that," Jane said.

"No. They said he didn't really talk about what he did out here." Jesse looked toward the cement floor. "I'm grateful you tipped Patrice off about the Creek guy, across the street."

Pip. Jane was glad Patrice had dug in on him.

"She was able to establish probable cause? To search his house?"

"She's working on it. In fact she was going to call you about visiting the flea market with her."

"So Pip is still a suspect?"

"Person of interest."

"FBI found the fake Waylon in the condo when they moved their guy in," Jane said. "Do you know— was the fake plant something that belonged to my deceased neighbor, Carl?"

"I don't know. Waylon's murder and the escaped convict situation are unrelated."

"So, why did the person who murdered Waylon leave a shirt in George's car?"

"Random choice to keep us chasing false leads. Maybe. Maybe the link has yet to be determined."

Jane nodded. She wasn't sure why Jesse had brought her in here. He hadn't really needed her expertise or her YouTube demo of beadmaking. He obviously had his own experts who matched the colors.

"Thanks for showing me this," she said.

Jane mourned this artist in his prime who had been murdered. Why? Because he found out Pip had been stealing his beads, making cheap and ugly imitations of his work? What about Randy, the married coffee guy? How did he fit in? Because Pip had not hidden the braid in her purse. It's possible he had a friend inside Winding Bayou who did it for him, but Jane doubted it.

Pip didn't seem like the type to have many friends. Also, Pip had not sent George that postcard from Jackson Prison. She shook her head, tired of trying to make sense of things that didn't fit into any discernable pattern.

"Was there something you wanted to ask me?"

Jesse was silent a beat. Two. Three. "No. I just wanted to show this to you before it all goes away. Get your take on things. You've been helpful." He paused a second. "And, you know, be careful. I don't like this braid being stashed in your handbag."

Jane worried now. Jesse thought she was in danger. Her expression must have revealed her jolt of fear, because Jesse added, "I'll make sure you're okay. With your permission, I can connect to your phone, so I'll always know your location."

"Really? Is that necessary?" She handed him her phone anyway.

"Password?"

She told him. He did something with the phones. Maybe a locator app where they were synced up. He handed her back her phone and showed her the app. "This is unofficial. You can delete it at any time."

"I'm fine with you knowing where I am. But will I know where you are at all times, too?"

Jesse laughed but didn't answer the question. Which was all the answer she needed. Despite herself, she was touched by his sensitivity in showing her the studio. His laugh was pretty great, too. There had been too little laughter in Jane's life lately.

"So is the whole police department going to know when I go grocery shopping?"

"No. Just me. And maybe Patrice?"

"Sure. Patrice is fine."

He locked up the door and handed the keys over to the guard on duty.

The guys shook hands while Jane stood amazed. She couldn't believe that she'd been the last civilian to see Waylon's studio in its original location. It was an honor, and she told Jesse that as they walked out to the front of the house.

"I thought you deserved to see his work space," Jesse told her.

Now it was Jane's turn to be speechless. Why was Jesse being so nice to her?

Chapter Nine

Just as Jesse had predicted, Patrice called Wednesday and asked for her help identifying any fake Waylon plants at the flea market.

"I figure Wednesday won't be as crowded as Saturday," Patrice said.

"Yeah. The crowd is lighter. What time?"

"Well, the flea market is next to the Cajun Café. Let's have lunch first. My treat."

"Thanks," Jane said. "I've never been."

"It's cute. Sits next to a body of water; they have a screened-in porch so you can watch the river flow. Excellent gumbo."

"Want to meet there?"

"No, I'll pick you up. Least I can do. In case you can't tell when I'm in uniform, I'm not really a flea market gal."

"Okay. Just text me when you get here, and I'll run down."

"Will do. Thanks again, Jane."

Jane had been to the flea market with her dad. He mostly stayed in a tented area with super cheap man-stuff, like tools and spark plugs. He'd filled a pink toolbox for her from his finds when she'd moved down, remarking that if she had any issues that required more than a screwdriver to call him. She didn't know exactly what a crescent wrench was for, but he'd put one in the cute toolbox. While Dad had been hunting good used tools for her, she'd explored the entire flea market. She came back and he was maybe five feet from where she'd left him, engrossed in an aisle full of packets of screws and nails. She'd know to skip that section with Patrice.

She read another section of the complicated grief book while she waited for Patrice. When her text pinged, she grabbed her bag and locked the door behind her. She was hungry. The Cajun Café wasn't crowded, and they got a table on the screened porch. Jane loved how authentically rustic this place was. It looked like it could be a hundred years old. But it was clean and nothing was worn except the silvered wood frames of the porch.

Patrice was in civilian clothes and she'd driven over in her own vehicle, so it felt more like friends meeting for lunch. Lunch was friendly, but not that simple. Jane asked Patrice about her kids.

"Well, they're in school till Thanksgiving holiday," Patrice said, whipping out her phone to show Jane pictures. Jane shared the latest photo of Little Suzy, standing in her crib, grabbing the rails, a smile showing pearly baby teeth. She was dressed to go out, in a pretty ivory dress and matching bow in her hair. She looked like a little angel.

"She's already walking."

"My daughter walked early too, compared to the boys."

Danny had walked at one year, but he was advanced in almost everything since the day he'd been born. Or maybe all moms thought that about their kids. Danny, however, was legit brilliant. He was currently on a project that picked ethical stocks. Smart with his heart in the right place. Jane didn't brag about Danny to Patrice, but she wanted to. Instead she talked about how Marisol's husband had gotten Suzy's first steps on video, so Jane got to see the moment Suzy lurched around the family corgi to get at a strawberry Marisol held out to her.

"She let go of the furniture in pursuit of fruit," Jane said, smiling.

Patrice laughed. "Is it hard that they live so far away?"

"It was at first," Jane said. "Well, it still is…their dad died six months ago. I worry about them. Still. And I crave Suzy like she's a cupcake."

"She's a cutie."

The server brought hot fresh-baked corn muffins. They dug in, and Jane noted the tang of jalapeno, or some other kind of spicy pepper. "This is so good," she said.

"Wait until you try your shrimp dish. It's my second favorite, next to gumbo."

They chewed for a few minutes in silence.

Jane came up for air and thought she smelled autumn waft in to the screened porch. "Am I crazy, or is the season changing?"

Patrice laughed, nodding her head. "Oh, yeah. It has been crisper these days." Patrice wore a sweater over a long-sleeved top. Jane was glad she'd grabbed her favorite jean jacket on the way out her door as her sleeves were short. She put it on, and Patrice laughed again. "Just like a real cracker," Patrice said.

Jane laughed, a little unsure of the connotation of "cracker" down here. In Detroit, it was a mildly negative word used to describe low-income white people. Jane didn't mind. She got it. Black people were called far worse every day by strangers on the street. She wondered if Patrice thought of herself as a cracker. Or did her Asian blood exempt her? Everyone called the houses on Orange Blossom "cracker" houses, and when she'd asked, Jane had been informed that "cracker" meant "old as dirt." She debated getting Patrice's take, but just then their lunches came out. Jane knew Patrice had not meant to insult her. She was saying Jane was one of them. Or almost like one of them. Patrice was sweet as pie. Maybe five years older than Marisol.

After she'd demolished half a plate of shrimp and rice, Jane asked Patrice a different question. "Do you get along with your mother?"

Patrice held up her index finger, indicating she'd answer after she swallowed her bite of food. "Woo, that's hot." Patrice fanned her face. "But so good."

The server had asked them for their heat level preferences. Jane got medium, but Patrice had opted for hot.

"My mom, she's super. She helped me so much when my kids were just babies. She still comes over a couple times a week, whenever I need her, and sometimes when I don't." Again the signature happy laugh.

Jane laughed too. "My mom was the same, and I feel bad I can't carry on that tradition for my daughter."

Patrice nodded. "Seems to be the way, even here. Lots of kids out of college moving west for tech jobs or east for finance. They go north for manufacturing now that Detroit seems to be on the upswing again."

Jane wondered if Patrice just made lucky guesses, or if she'd been researched. She nodded. Of course the police were going to check her out before they'd ask her to help on a case, even in an advisory capacity. That was fine.

They split the bill again, and Patrice drove next door to the vast flea market parking lot, which was grassland roped off in neat rows.

"Glad I wore my sneakers," Patrice said.

Jane had worn flip-flops the first time and regretted it, so she too was in her favorite walkers, navy blue with hot pink laces.

"The entrance area has the fruit and veg vendors. Tools and light bulbs and whatnot over there." Jane pointed out the canvas pop-up stores her dad was so crazy about. "The big barn is where the crafters have booths." They walked toward the white barn with the black roof.

"I might get some produce on our way out," Patrice remarked. "My kids love strawberries."

Jane was still a bit in awe of how abundant fresh fruit and veggies were, even this late in the year. They passed people who opted to lay a few trinkets on blankets and, sometimes, tables. Inside the barn, things were more formal. This was where the good stuff was, if you considered tacky fake plants "good." Jane admitted there were nice things in here. She bought a lovely quilt patterned in soft pink and green, the colors of her Desert Rose dishes that had sparked the whole front of the house color scheme. She could picture cuddling up with it in December on her white sofa. The vendor agreed to hold the quilt until they came back around.

"Sorry," Jane said as they walked around the outer perimeter of the barn, going slow, checking out the center aisle, too.

"No worries," Patrice said. "It will look great in your living room. You're great at mixing eclectic styles."

"Thanks," Jane said, her gaze landing on the center aisle, where Pip had set up shop on a long table with a cash box and an array of fake Waylons. "Look, Patrice. Center aisle."

"Yeah, I saw it too. Let's walk down the aisle a bit and then turn around, catch him unaware if we can."

Jane felt a little like a secret agent. Also, a little afraid. Pip didn't like her, and he didn't even know her. But she bolstered her courage by remembering he was almost as small as she was. She could probably take him. Ha. Well, she could sit on him. They made their way slowly around the aisle and up the center.

As they got closer, Jane noticed that Pip seemed to be doing brisk business. When they were one table down, she saw why. "Genuine Dead NDN Beads!" read the sign. Jane was indignant on Waylon's behalf. Just then someone asked for a selfie with Pip. Jane rolled her eyes, but Patrice was focused and slowly moving in for the kill.

They were able to blend easily with the small fan club Pip had gathered. Jane even picked up and inspected a few of the atrocious copycats. They looked like Waylon's beads, just as advertised, although the gobs of glue and the sickly green color of the plant leaves took away some of the luster. "These are Waylon's beads. He's even got some on here that Waylon hadn't used for the installation," Jane whispered and discreetly pointed to the green beads.

Patrice motioned for Jane to move on to the next booth. There had been some chatter on the internet with photos of Jane labeled "Local art expert says Waylon's the real deal." Jane moved back behind a small group of people paying, walking on to the next booth, which featured local honey as well as pottery honey pots. She moved on to the next table. It featured knitted toilet paper roll cozies and needlepoint toilet seat covers. She turned slightly to see Patrice buying two fake Waylons. Pip didn't seem to recognize her. Perhaps they'd had minimal contact. Patrice took her time checking out the honey lady, then caught up with Jane.

"Let's get your quilt and my strawberries and head out. You can look at the sample of Pip's wares when we get to the car."

"Roger that," Jane said, even though no crime novel she'd ever read had included those words.

A quarter of an hour later, in the bright sunlight, Jane was able to say with some certainty that the beads had been made by Waylon.

"Aside from the green beads and the sign advertising them as such, how can you tell these are Waylon's beads?"

"Size, for one thing. But the other colors, well, now that I've seen the studio and examined the beads, it's color. Size and color."

"Okay." Patrice started the car and pulled out of the parking lot. "That should be good enough to get a search warrant. I snapped a photo of the incriminating sign, too."

Jane felt a chill that had nothing to do with the autumn air. They might have just found Waylon's killer.

Chapter Ten

Barb Stone's second day in Florida started with the stale taste of a good dream gone bad. She drank motel room coffee to wash the bad away and went over the facts so far. Yesterday, she'd visited Dorothy Donaldsin. Next, she participated in a search of the woman's house that yielded some disturbing information that did not align with Dorothy's story. Another agent questioned Dorothy for the second time, because Barb kept a priority meet with George. She hadn't told him that somehow, some way, with no known friends or contacts outside of prison, without being flagged by any airline, Louie Donaldsin had made it to Clearwater, Florida, shortly before or after Barb had arrived herself.

Agents had checked both Tampa and the smaller St. Pete and Clearwater airports, as they had all the way down the I-75 corridor from Detroit. No member of any airline personnel had been able to identify Louie Donaldsin as being on any flight from the time he walked off the prison farm until the time they had him in Clearwater eating a pizza he'd taken the time to remove from his mother's freezer and bake, likely during the time he'd taken a shower in his mother's guest bathroom. He was possibly no longer in Clearwater. He had obviously had help from the minute he walked off the prison farm. An unknown criminal crony or organization had facilitated his every step. The FBI did not sit well with unknowns. Duffy brought even more agents in on the case to fan out the airport search and look into private aircraft.

"Barb, if you capture Donaldsin and can turn him the way you did George Sanders, we may be able to reel in some bigger fish," Duffy had said on the phone last night.

Barb read the final report on Dorothy Donaldsin as she finished her coffee. Dorothy ("Call me Dot," she'd asked the second agent, the one who had not put her son behind bars) feigned cognitive impairment, changing her story from her statement at Barb's initial visit, saying that yes, of course, her son had visited her, though he had not checked in at the visitor's desk and there were no images of him on security cameras. Dorothy had reaffirmed Louie was a good boy. Naturally, she'd given him a key to her house. But, no, she didn't know his current location. She assumed he'd gone back to prison. He'd had special permission to visit her, Dot continued to claim.

This mess was on her, Barb knew. As far as they could calculate, Louie was at Dorothy's while Barb got Dorothy's false statement. Barb had assumed, incorrectly, that it would take Donaldsin longer to arrive in Clearwater. So had Duffy back in Detroit, but once he'd given her the go, she knew the bust was hers to make and own. She brushed her teeth and dressed in jeans and a T-shirt. She threw a pair of cuffs and a can of pepper spray into the go-bag designed to look like a large purse. She kept her FBI issue Glock, as always when not sleeping or showering, in a side holster. She would not blend in Florida during a sultry October wearing a jacket to conceal her weapon, but that's what dark boxy shirts were for.

She poured a to-go coffee into the too-small cup and threw her jacket and other change of clothes into the carry-on and left the building, already considering her next step as she moved into the parking lot.

The help Donaldsin would need to accomplish such a mission was private jet level. Scary big money had to be behind his escape. As soon as she found that out yesterday, she'd had Tom Benton from the Tampa office placed on duty one door down from George. She hoped her reluctant informer would be safe. As it turned out, George had been smart to be spooked by that postcard. Now if he could just keep himself alive until she captured Donaldsin, everyone could get back to their lives. She threw the overnight bag into the trunk and sank into the driver's seat of her vehicle for the duration.

The car started right up, but things were bumpy for Barb this morning, despite the adequate five hours of sleep, the hot shower, the coffee. She knew the challenge had been her vivid dream. She'd been with George inside a shopping mall that was also a hotel, in the weird way dreams had of combining images that never happened in waking hours. They'd walked, holding hands, past the display of designer handbags. They'd evaded a woman pursuing them with clouds of perfume. And they'd ended up in front of a jewelry store, bending over a glass case, looking at diamond rings. Barb awakened with a deep sense of love and peace, the kind of peace that could only be found after a work situation had been resolved or love had been made.

Neither of those things had happened, although that feeling stayed with her. Even now, it pierced her and invaded her mind, a mind that needed, for George's sake, to be focused only on capturing Donaldsin. She pointed her vehicle south on Gulf Boulevard. She headed toward St. Pete, calling in to the team en route.

Donaldsin, she heard, was on the move. One possible sighting at a gas station close to Indian Rocks Beach, more information forthcoming.

"I'm outside Indian Rocks right now," Barb told the team. "Heading to St. Pete."

"We have him going south on Gulf Boulevard."

"As am I." She debated turning east and onto the freeway in Largo, the route Google Maps suggested, but then, with this added intel, decided to stick to Gulf Boulevard. It wasn't high season, so the ride flowed like the water sparkling outside her car window. Unwilling to be distracted by the beautiful shoreline for more than a few seconds, she called Benton and soon enough wished she had not. He told a long story about a potted plant and two civilian woman who had seen Benton in George's condo.

"He blew my cover," Benton whined.

"Relax. They're his friends. Names Jane and Kim?"

"Yeah." Benton refused to be mollified. "Even the local PD got involved," Benton added.

"Don't sweat it," Barb advised. "This is not the first time their hometown homicide has bumped into our case. They're separate entities." She stifled the urge to ask Benton how George was holding up, instead she mentioned the sighting at Indian Rocks and told him to stay with George.

"Where are you?" Benton wanted to know.

"I'm on Gulf Boulevard, just past Largo."

"Hoh boy."

"What?"

"It's just a more complicated way to come into St. Pete," Benton said. "More water than land. Lots of barrier islands, the Intracoastal, Tampa Bay, beaches in every little town, of which there are many. Don't confuse St. Pete Beach with St. Pete, the city. St. Pete Beach is west of the city."

"Thanks," Barb said.

She disconnected, freeing her personal bandwidth to scan for a light-colored SUV. She felt the sharp pain of a stress migraine starting on the right side of her prefrontal cortex. She needed every inch of her brain's real estate to be on task. She needed painkillers, more coffee, and a tourist map. She pulled over at a coffee shop in Reddington Beach, which she hoped would provide all three. This patch of the Gulf was wall-to-wall mansions interspersed with high-rise condos. Parking was hidden from view. The make and model of the car with a partial license plate came through before she even ordered her coffee. Great. 2019 American-made in Opal White. Every other vehicle on the road, not to mention the parking lot she was currently cruising, was some variation of white SUV. Also, no drive-through. She pulled into a spot behind the building.

****

It took three stops, but eventually Barb found the kind of tourist map she needed at a touristy shopping mall on Treasure Island. The outdoor mall had a restaurant facing the Gulf and the causeway from the mainland. Barb was able to secure a booth with an optimal window view just after the lunch rush diminished. She presented her badge as she spoke with the manager about doing discreet surveillance for a few hours.

The woman appeared to hesitate.

Barb brought out her tourist map and monocular from behind the large shopping bag from one of the more high-end stores at the mall. She'd purchased some beach attire while she left wallet-sized photos of Donaldsin and her card with each store manager. She'd done it all the way from Reddington Beach, hitting up hotels, restaurants, and now this outdoor shopping mall. She had several shopping bags she'd already placed on the opposite seat.

"This is all I'll be using," Barb said, lifting the monocular. "I assure you, nobody will notice. I'll order lunch and request my server to keep the coffee coming. I need to study this"—Barb pointed to the map—"as any tourist would."

"I'm Lisa. Just getting off shift," the manager said. "I'll stay over and wait on you personally. That should take care of any concerns the night manager might have."

"Thank you," Barb said. "I'll have the grouper sandwich and a salad."

"Right away," Lisa said.

When Lisa came back with a cup of coffee, Barb saw she'd slipped into a server's white shirt and black slacks. Lisa winked as she set the coffee down to the side of the unfolded map.

Barb sipped the coffee, her not-so-secret weapon, as she studied the map. She'd only canvassed two beach communities before Treasure Island. Other agents would scour the remainder of the area. Despite the number of eyes devoted to this manhunt, there had not been another sighting of the white SUV. Barb began memorizing the Gulf beaches. Sunset Beach was just a minute down the road, over the bridge. She checked her own location, which sat next to another body of water. The Intracoastal. She noted that there were far fewer restaurants and hotels east of the Intracoastal. It was more a residential area. She committed the area to memory. There would be alleys and little crooked lanes that the map didn't identify. That was always the way. But at least she could be assured she'd know the main streets. Lisa came with her sandwich, and Barb realized she still had not touched her salad. She smiled and folded the map so Lisa could set down her meal. She was hungry, several cups of coffee being the only sustenance she'd had today. She needed to fuel up for the fight ahead. They were close to catching Donaldsin; she could almost taste it.

Chapter Eleven

Fred was chatting with another man as Jane neared the mailboxes, which meant that their postal carrier had recently delivered all the junk mail, which is all he usually delivered these days, unless she had a package from an online retailer. She had her bank automatically pay her bills. As she got closer, she saw the guy Fred was talking to was Rich. Fred should be doing handyman things like keeping Big Snapper out of the pool area, but his biggest job seemed to be chatting up the residents.

"Hi," Jane said, opening her slot and gathering out the vast array of sale papers and envelopes with no return addresses. She shoved it all into her canvas bag to sort later. She wanted to ask Fred something, but she hoped Rich would leave first. He didn't.

"How're you today, Janey?" Fred asked. Rich smirked. She didn't like the nickname, but it wasn't important enough to mention. Rich was the kind of guy, that, if he knew she didn't like the name, would take much more delight in saying it each time he saw her.

"I'm fine, but listen." Rich was too nosy to leave, and maybe he knew something. He lived in the first-floor corner unit a few feet from the mailboxes.

"All ears," Fred said.

"Do you know who rented 205?"

Both men glanced up. All the shades were drawn,

as usual, in 205. But Jane had seen two men going in with a key just as she came down. They'd been carrying bags from the Piggly Wiggly, and both wore jackets and sharply creased dress pants.

"Those mobsters?" Rich said. Then he added, "Kidding."

Fred laughed. "We hear George has a babysitter in 203."

"So it makes complete sense that the mob is in 205."

The two men yukked it up like they were the funniest guys on earth.

Jane mentally rolled her eyes. But at least she'd gleaned that management was aware of the two very quiet and overdressed renters now checked in to 205. She turned and walked away without saying goodbye. The guys were still laughing.

Kim came out her back door as Jane walked toward the stairwell. Jane and Kim had a habit of meeting around the mailbox this time every day.

"How's poor George?" Kim said.

"Awful," Jane answered. "Heartbroken."

"We should cheer him up," Kim said. "Have you been to the Boat House yet? Chilled wine and Catch of the Day."

"No. Where is it?"

"On the Intracoastal. Sunset's spectacular. No beach. Boat slips." Kim looked at her watch. "Ever since the clocks fell back, sunset is earlier than ever. Get George, and we'll go over there. They've got a band, too. We can show George our line dance moves."

"What about Benton?"

"Well, George isn't a prisoner, is he?"

"No." Jane hadn't seen much of George since Benton had arrived on scene. "I'll give him a call."

Kim headed to the mailbox and her fan club. Jane pulled out her phone and called George on the way upstairs. He didn't answer, but as she passed his door, he opened it and stepped out.

"What have you done?" Jane said, eyeing George's new, and very bright, blond hair. "I liked your brown hair!"

"Shhh," George said. "Let's go before Benton sees me. We've got to take your car. Mine's got that tracking thingy on it. And I left my phone at home." He was already heading for the elevator. Jane followed. From the back, his hair looked even more impossibly blonde. They rode the elevator to a deserted hallway, walked to the door to Jane's garage. She started to open it, but George whispered, "Wait."

Jane sighed.

"Call Kim. She can meet us down here or drive herself."

Jane thought Kim might be back from the mailboxes if her dueling swains had run out of compliments. She was. Jane explained they were leaving now, Kim said okay, and Jane held the door to her garage open a crack until she saw Kim come down the hall.

"What are we all doing in your garage?" Kim said.

"Avoiding Benton," George said.

Jane turned on the light, and Kim saw George.

"Yikes! What happened to your hair?"

"I went to your stylist, and she gave me the Kim color job," George said.

"Ha ha," Kim said.

Jane preferred George's dark hair, but at least he'd had the sense to go to a salon.

"I suppose you think that disguise will throw the Detroit Mob off your trail," Kim said. She opened the passenger door and got in front. "Shotgun," she said to George before slamming her door.

George got in back and slunk down low in the seat.

"For gosh sake," Kim said. "Nobody's gonna see you."

"Benton," Jane said, turning the wheel and heading toward the gate.

"Take Bay Pines to that new Food Fare on Pendleton. Just over the bridge."

Jane didn't say anything. There were bridges everywhere around here, but she knew where the Food Fare was. She liked their organic wine.

"I'm so glad to get out of those four walls!" George said, straightening up in his seat. "Barb hasn't called."

"You call her?" Kim asked.

"No."

"There you go," Kim said.

"You think I should?"

"Wouldn't hurt," Kim said. "Turn here. Okay, now next to that hotel, pull in the parking lot."

Jane found a spot and pulled in.

"We're early, but the band's been playing since noon," Kim said.

"Is this it?" Jane asked. A tiny little one-story building sat between a high-rise hotel and a very large mansion surrounded by hedges taller than people.

"Good story," Kim said. "The mayor used to own this town. Literally. That's his house next door. And the

Boat House was his actual boat house. Then he got into some financial trouble, maybe dipping into civic funds, but whatever, he was fined millions. He had to sell off his property and resign from his job. The only thing he kept was his mansion next door and this little bit of land."

Jane looked at the huge parking lot for the little boat house turned restaurant.

"Anyway, it's a kind of poor man's yacht club. You need to buy a membership. And the former mayor gets to approve or deny membership. For, you know, folks like us. I have my card right in my purse." Kim laughed, and so did Jane. George stayed silent.

"We're safe as houses," Kim promised as they locked up the car and headed into the Boat House. Inside, the place wasn't much. Kind of like a big barn with a low ceiling and long banquet tables and plastic chairs. Except for the busy bar area, the inside was empty. A waitress walked by, heading to the deck with a tray full of drinks in plastic cups.

Kim led them outside, where a band played and the round umbrella tables were about half full. They chose one with a water view. "Nice," Jane said, deciding to ignore all the plastic.

"Busted," George said.

Benton had been sitting at the bar, but once George spotted him, he came over, pulled out the last chair, and sat. "Hey, Kim," Benton said.

Kim smiled and blushed before showing her club card to the waitress, who took a picture of it.

"How'd you find me?"

"I'm good at my job," Benton said.

"So I did this to my hair for nothing?"

"I like it," Benton said.

"Do you really have to sit with us?" George sulked. "I need a little space. It feels like I'm suffocating!"

"Bring him a double bourbon," Kim said to the waitress, pointing at George.

"Okay, so that's two white wines, a beer, and a double bourbon. Rocks?"

"No rocks," Jane and George said at the same time.

"Listen, buddy," Benton said. "I hear you. And the hair is good. Smart. I think we're fairly safe here. It's a private club; you look like you just got off one of those fancy boats."

Everyone looked to the boats in the slips on the water. Jane took in George's pink golf shirt with white sweater tied around his shoulders. She looked under the table and sure enough he had those boat shoes with no socks on. And white jeans. Jane looked up again. George was tanned, but not too much. He was playing the greatest role of his life.

"So I'm gonna just sit at the bar and let you enjoy the company of these lovely ladies." Benton was looking at Kim as he said it, but Jane was getting used to it. Everybody loved Kim. Even Jane.

"Thanks," George said as Benton sauntered away. "I will relax as soon as I get my drinks."

Benton left and Jane looked at Kim. "Wasn't that beer for Benton?"

"Nope," George said, taking the beer the server handed him along with the double bourbon. "Daddy needs a drink or two tonight."

Jane and Kim toasted with their wine as the sun made its way down the sky. The band started playing the inexplicably popular Beach Boys song "Kokomo."

Jane preferred early Beach Boys, but when in Rome.

Everyone quenched their thirst. Kim held up her wine glass to Benton, and he saluted her with what looked like vodka but could be water.

"What exciting things have you guys been doing since we last saw ourselves?" Jane asked. She wanted to speak to Benton alone. Fred and Rich may have been joking, but it wouldn't hurt to tell him what they'd said about the "mobsters" in 205. She just didn't want George to hear. He was spooked enough already.

George sipped bourbon with one hand and checked the location of the sun, his other hand shading his eyes. "Gonna be a while yet until sundown."

"I've been reading all day," Jane said, not remarking on the sun, which she was starting to take for granted. Back in Michigan, the skies would be slate and the air cold.

"How's the book?" George asked, beginning to unwind as his double cocktail worked magic.

"Good," Jane said. She didn't say that the murder had happened on page three. Or that the killer was a hit man with a vendetta. Too on the nose for George.

"This place is so cool," George said. "I was at the salon all day. Got a mani-pedi while I waited for the color to process."

Jane thought George would fit right in in L.A.

"What about you, Kim?"

"Cleaning." Kim's nickname with the widows was "Mrs. Clean." Jane wished she could think of a way to hire her without it being insulting.

"Really? You haven't been anywhere?"

"I'm here now," Kim said. "Oh. Look at the pirate ship. I took my grandson on that last time he came up from Sarasota."

Jane was a tiny bit jealous of Kim having her grandkids so close.

George asked about grandkids, and both Kim and Jane pulled up photos on their phones and passed them around. Jane missed little Suzy like a limb.

"How come your son doesn't have any kids?" George asked.

"Too soon. He's only been married a year," Jane said.

"Let them have some fun first. Babies are a lot of work," George said.

Jane and Kim looked at each other and laughed.

"What?" George said.

"How the hell would you know?" Kim asked George.

"I'm the oldest of six, and I did everything from changing diapers to walking the floor with a crying kid at two a.m."

"Oh. That's sweet," Kim said, showing a photo of Justina, her youngest granddaughter, only a year old but already walking. In the photo, Justina was trying to push an airport cart loaded with the family's luggage. "His family's from Nebraska, so they go out there during hurricane season." Jane took the phone from George.

George laughed. "Gotta say, I love kids."

"Does Barb want kids? Can an FBI agent even have children?"

"It's easier for the men to have families, I think," George said. He didn't respond to the first part of Kim's question, and nobody pressured him about that.

Jane and Kim stashed their phones in their purses.

George looked thoughtful. The server arrived with their fish, and everyone said yes to another round of drinks.

Jane was quiet, chewing on a french fry. George looked sad. See, she thought, this is what love does. It turns you into some romance zombie.

George took another hefty swallow of his bourbon, and Jane figured he was building liquid courage.

George soon looked relaxed, as if he had not a care in the world. "I didn't tell you guys," he said. "You know the Indian murder?" That's what the papers had been calling Waylon's murder. "A guy I work with, I drove him home today, and his yard was all decked out same way as Waylon's was."

"Oh, wow," Kim said.

"Why didn't you tell us?" Jane asked.

"I called the homicide detective on the case," George said.

"Jesse Singer." Kim said it like a statement.

"Yeah. He's going to look into it."

"When did this happen?"

"Just yesterday. I was going to tell you guys, but I got the idea about doing my hair and buying some Florida outfits."

"Well, you're telling us now."

Kim reached across George and grabbed Jane's hand. She gave it a squeeze and said, "Singer's okay. He'll check it out, and eventually they'll get this guy. You can trust him."

"I feel safe with all the FBI around," George said. "What I don't get is why whoever murdered Waylon put that shirt in my car. I thought for sure it was the Detroit mob, but Benton says no."

"It's too bad the FBI can't help with the Waylon

thing," Kim said. "Not that Singer won't find the killer." She stuck a big chunk of fish into her mouth and chewed.

"Two crimes. Two separate stories. Does that seem weird to you?" Jane asked them as she gratefully accepted a fresh glass of wine from the waitress.

"You mean, maybe not a coincidence?" George said.

"Maybe not."

"Barb is here in an official capacity. She'll get to the bottom of it. Or Singer will."

George crammed more fries in his mouth that Jane thought humanly possible. Nobody really wanted to talk about the murder or the escaped convict.

After dinner, Jane and Kim sipped Bailey's and George had more bourbon as they watched the coral sun dip into the pinked rippling water at the horizon. Always amazing. Every single time. Except those rare days when clouds covered up the show.

Benton opened the door for them. They passed through the Boat House to get to the parking lot. Still pretty empty, but a woman was setting up for karaoke. At that door, Benton held up a hand and said he'd go outside first. It had gotten dark fast.

"Well, we never did any dancing," Kim said.

"Want to take a walk in the morning?" Jane asked. Kim had a Fitbit, and she fretted if she didn't get her steps in.

"Good idea," Kim said.

They were about halfway to the car when they heard a loud crack. Jane looked around for lightning.

"Get down!" Benton had his weapon out as he gave the low command. "That was a gunshot."

Chapter Twelve

Benton crouched and they mimicked his movement. Everybody crab-walked to Jane's car. More shots rang out.

"George," Benton said, "Keep these ladies behind the engine. Safest place for you all right now."

"Where are you going?" George said, but he herded Jane and Kim as instructed.

From behind their steel shield, Jane called Jesse. "We're at the Boat House. Parking lot. Somebody's shooting at us."

"On our way," Jesse said.

"One shooter, over there." Benton pointed toward the road close to the mansion. "The car is in his way. Just keep your heads down below the windows." He smushed heads down.

"Cops are on their way," Jane said.

"Thanks, Jane. I think he's gone," Benton said after scouting both ends of George's car. "But Jane's tires have been slashed," he added.

Jane thought that was weird. Somebody came up to the Boat House, slashed her tires, and then went back to the hedge next to the road to shoot them. Well, maybe he wanted to make sure they wouldn't get away. She hoped Jesse would be here soon.

Jane noticed human voices. Management and maybe other customers had come out to the parking lot.

Next to her, Kim was rummaging through her purse. She pulled out a gun twice the size of her hand. George was whispering that maybe they should get the weapon out of the glove box.

"I don't own a firearm," Jane said.

George and Kim turned amazed faces toward hers.

"This is Florida, everybody owns a gun," Kim said.

Jane was glad the cops and FBI were on her side. Benton popped his head up and quickly back down. Nobody shot at him.

"Stand down," Benton yelled to a waitress holding a gun aimlessly a few yards from the car. "You three stay here."

Benton ran out sideways, his gun pointed east, away from the waitress and the bass player from the band, who also had a gun out. All was quiet, as far as bullets went. Jane guessed Benton was right, and the assailant had fled. All the other civilians filed back into the restaurant like this was a normal thing that happened every day.

George looked at Jane. "I'm not sure if it's me or you they're gunning for," he said. Jane thought maybe the shooter had been aiming for both of them, but she didn't say anything until she heard the sirens.

"Jesse's here," she said.

"Barb!" George sprinted out from behind the car and toward the mansion.

Jane and Kim looked at each other. "Stay here," Jane said.

"Not going anywhere," Kim assured her. "What the hell is George doing?"

Kim didn't swear, not usually. She had to be terrified. Jane was okay because Jesse was here and he'd take care of them. Sure enough, Patrice was soon by their side, leading them into the restaurant, using herself and her gun as shields against any bullets. One shot rang out before they got to the door. George's bright hair had been visible next to the mansion's hedge and then it wasn't. Jane screamed. "George!"

Kim grabbed one arm, and Patrice got the door and Jane's other arm. "You can't go out there, Jane. We'll make sure George is okay."

"He's got blond hair now, Patrice."

"Good to know. You two stay inside. This will all be over very soon."

Jane and Kim walked into the Boat House. Everyone was sitting at the long tables, even the karaoke lady. There were chains on the doors leading out to the deck, floodlights trained on the boats in their slips. They found two seats, and someone brought them coffee.

Chapter Thirteen

After a few hours at the restaurant, Barb had the map to St. Pete and its surrounding areas memorized. She was most interested in Madeira Beach, the residential section northeast of Treasure Island. It seemed the logical place for Donaldsin to try to hole up for the night or to make his way toward St. Pete via Tyrone Boulevard.

From her server at the restaurant, Barb had learned the Veteran's Affairs building on Tyrone kept track of a large homeless population. She said they allowed all vets who refused housing to camp on the extensive property. Donaldsin could blend in. From the VA on Tyrone, a quick turn east would get him to downtown St. Pete. George's condo building was west of downtown.

Barb cruised the residential area east of the Intracoastal. She had her earpiece in place and communicated her location to Benton. He updated her that the team had mobilized around the same area that was Barb's focus. An alert had been posted on local television. St. Pete PD put out an online and televised alert with a warning and Donaldsin's description plus a central hotline number. Everything was in place. Residents in the area had been warned to stay inside until the wanted fugitive, presumed armed and dangerous, had been apprehended. Many of the larger homes, and one enormous mansion, were unoccupied. It was out of season for rich folks, although the heat, even as the sun began to go down, felt more than adequate to Barb.

Then Benton said he was on the move, following George. He gave the plate number of the car Jane Chasen was driving. There was a third passenger.

"Kim?"

"Yes. They as yet are unaware I'm following."

Barb spotted a man in a dark hoodie walking down the street. Most residents had obeyed the strong suggestion to stay indoors. She passed the guy but couldn't get an ID from her rearview mirror. She circled around the block and parked several houses down from the lone wolf in the hoodie. She got out of her vehicle and followed him on foot, shoving plastic cuffs into the back pocket of her blue jean capris.

Benton confirmed their arrival at a small restaurant tucked between a mansion and a six-story hotel. Seaside Tower. Barb pinpointed the hotel from the map in her mind.

"I'm following them in. Sitting at the bar next to the exit while they order. Okay, going over."

"I'm on foot, By the Beach sub, following a lone pedestrian, male, dark hoodie." She gave the cross streets.

Barb heard Benton talking to George, Jane, and Kim, each of whom he identified by name.

Barb searched the map again in her mind's eye. There had not been a Boat House restaurant in the area. There had been a hotel, Seaside Tower, and then a mansion.

She followed well behind her lone wolf. They were

deep inside a middle-class suburb as the sun kept sinking. He had been talking on his phone and then suddenly quickened his pace. Barb didn't think he'd spotted her. They were heading toward the outer perimeter of the subdivision now. He could walk up to any house and get out his key and enter. She was half expecting that. But after another thirty minutes, just as the top floors of a hotel came into view, the lone wolf stopped at a mansion with tall hedges. He looked around the corner. Barb was almost a block behind him. She quickened her pace.

Though her earpiece, she heard Benton's words, "Shots fired," at the same time she heard gunshots and screams and sirens, all seemingly at once until time slowed as it did when things were coming to a head.

"Suspect in range," she said as she saw Donaldsin's profile. That hook nose was a dead giveaway. He stood at the edge of the shrubbery where it cornered with the contours of the mansion grounds. He lowered the hand holding the firearm to his side. She edged closer to him. Then George's voice yelled her name.

She yelled louder, at Donaldsin. "FBI. Drop your weapon."

But Donaldsin was already firing the first of three shots he got off in the seconds it took for Barb to reach him where he pushed into the hedges. The attempt to escape was futile as sturdy fencing hid behind the hedge, and the Glock in her hand, aimed at him, made his escape impossible.

"Drop your weapon, Donaldsin!"

Donaldsin froze. She'd shoot him in the leg if he didn't do it now. Shoot to kill was not a declarative in this case, but if he'd shot George, oh, she'd be tempted.

"FBI. Drop your weapon *now*!" As she yelled the command, Benton came up behind Donaldsin and ripped the weapon from the convict's hand.

"Hands up," Benton barked. Donaldsin, out of options, obeyed.

"Sorry, Barb. Your CI got away from me," Benton said.

Barb didn't have time to process that information before more law enforcement arrived.

"Detective Jesse Singer, St. Pete homicide," the second guy said, holding out an evidence bag for Benton. Benton nodded, and they secured Donaldsin's weapon.

A uniformed female officer spoke to Singer, shaking her head as Barb holstered her weapon and cuffed Donaldsin.

"Officer Patrice Riley," Singer said, after Barb finished the arrest protocol.

"Agent Stone," Riley said, "there's one man down, ambulance on the way. I'm sorry. It's your CI George Sanders."

Barb wanted to take the butt of her weapon and wipe the smirk off Donaldsin's face.

Singer spoke up next. "We've got the temporary command center downtown. A cell with Donaldsin's name on it. Shall we transport the prisoner?"

"Yes. We'll meet you there soon, detective," Barb said. "Thank you both for your work."

As they escorted Donaldsin away, Barb told Benton to start on the witness statements. She heard the ambulance before she saw it and walked in slow motion around the corner and into the parking lot. A fire truck's lights were flashing and two men were working on George. Or, no. It wasn't George. The man on the ground, bleeding profusely, was a blond. Two more marked cars were at the doors of the little shack of a restaurant squeezed between the mansion and the hotel. Nobody else was on the ground. Barb walked right up to the bleeding man.

"FBI." She pulled out her badge for EMS personnel and slapped it open without taking her eyes off George. Because it was George, she saw now. His eyes were closed and his hair was the wrong color, but it was George. She dropped to her knees in the pool of blood surrounding her informant and took his hand. "How did you know I was there?"

George's eyes fluttered open. "I knew if Donaldsin was here, you wouldn't be far behind him," he said. When he closed his eyes again, his head fell sideways, like he was sleeping. And then she had to back away because they were loading George into an ambulance.

"Mercy," said one of the guys who'd worked on George. His arms were red up to his elbows, and the metallic smell of blood was thick in the air.

"What?" Barb asked.

"Mercy Hospital. That's where we're taking him. Are you coming?"

"Yes," she said. As she waited for George to be loaded, she called Duffy in Detroit. "We got Donaldsin. Temporary command post St. Pete police station. Benton's talking to witnesses. My CI was hit. I'm going to the hospital in the ambulance with him."

"You need to get to St. Pete PD and start turning Donaldsin."

"It won't hurt him to cool his heels in lock-up."

Barb clicked her phone off before Duffy could reply and got into the back of the ambulance with George.

She felt something tear inside her chest, wanting out.

George was too pale and still unconscious, but EMS had stopped the flowing blood. That had to be good. Someone worked across from her, giving George something intravenously.

Barb bent down close to his ear. "If you live, I'll tell you a secret."

She prayed for him to wake up and talk again. This was her fault. She'd talked him into signing on to this, even though he didn't want to do it. He'd pleaded with her. She'd ignored him. She'd used him. For the damn FBI. Twelve years in a career that was mostly paperwork and stakeouts that yielded little to nothing. If she'd been a minute closer to the scene, would George still be whole? Would he be standing there in the parking lot while she gave him shit about coloring his hair?

"Stop it," she told herself.

"Huh? Pardon?" the EMS guy said. He had a woman's voice. Barb noticed then that it was a woman.

"Nothing," Barb said.

The EMS woman was busy checking George's vitals and didn't respond other than to say, "It's fine to hold his hand. Just don't jar the IV."

George's right hand had been placed on his chest, above where the bullet wound had been dressed. Barb carefully lifted his hand and enfolded it between both of hers.

The FBI, her job, had done this. "I'm so sorry," she said, even though George didn't hear her. She thought about her career highlights. Tonight was another one. Every win she'd ever had she owed to George. She'd been undercover when she arrested him. She'd turned him into an informer who put away a lot of bad guys. And then, when he tried to straighten out his life, she reeled him in again. Against his will. This was all down to her. If the medical professionals could fix George, she could fix everything else.

Chapter Fourteen

Jane was worried about George. Despite all the coffee she'd automatically been swallowing, she was so tired. Being interrogated by two different government agencies had wrung her out. The police had impounded her car. Donaldsin had to have been the one who slashed her tires, so it made sense that the car was part of a crime scene. Kim called Rich, and he'd come to pick them up.

Whatever Kim and Rich had talked about in the front seat, Jane didn't hear from the back. There had been an overflow of words at the Boat House after the shooting. Her brain couldn't hold any more words. They all spilled out before she could decode them. She felt drugged, even though the wine she'd had must have worn off long ago. What time was it? She pulled out her phone. 2 a.m. When they got to the Bayou, Jane said goodnight to Kim and Rich. She told Kim she didn't think she was up to a walk in the morning and told Rich thanks for the ride. Rich had his arm around Kim. They said goodnight, and Jane walked up the stairs alone.

She was so tired, but she couldn't sleep. She took a hot shower. Still, sleep wouldn't come. She probably had way too much coffee. Why wasn't Barb calling her? Oh. Jane went to her desk and found Barb's card, the one George had given her that first day, when they met. She paced the rooms, punched the number into her contacts and heard the phone ring and ring. Barb's voice said to leave a message, so Jane left a message. "How's George? How are you? This is Jane. Please call me."

She settled on her sofa and closed her eyes. She put the Calm App on her phone and tried to rest to the sound of ocean waves. If she couldn't sleep, at least she could rest.

The phone woke her at 4 a.m. Barb.

"How is he?" Jane refused to believe George was gone.

"He'll live," Barb said. "Donaldsin was a lousy shot. Only one bullet hit him on the left side. Didn't hit anything vital."

"Are you okay? Where are you?"

"I'm heading over to George's place. I have his house key, figure I might as well stay there."

"If you can't sleep, come next door. I'm up."

"Thanks. I'll see you later."

****

Jane did sleep, off and on. Jesse called at 6 a.m. to check on her.

"Have you been to sleep yet?" Jane asked.

"No. Just going home, now. Hey, I want to see you."

"Why? Okay? When? Did you hear, George is not going to die, I mean, someday, sure, like all the rest of us, but not yet?"

Jane knew she was babbling.

"I'm glad George will be okay," Jesse said. "But this is about Waylon. George called in on the guy he works with who has an installation in his yard. I'd like you to look it over and get your opinion. And again, such good news about George."

"Yes. It's good news. And yes, I'll look at the yard." Silence on the line.

"Get some rest," Jesse finally said.

"You too."

"We'll talk this afternoon?" Jesse said.

"Yes. Call me."

They hung up, and Jane cranked up the air. She'd put on a brushed flannel nightgown after her shower, just for the comforting feel of the soft material. It was as close to a hug as she was gonna get right now.

"Alexa, play 'Dancing in the Dark.' "

Alexa started the Rhianna song. Jane went and changed into jeans and a cotton tee. She'd meant Bruce Springsteen, but oh well. This is what getting old feels like, she guessed.

Her phone pinged with a text.

—*You up?*—It was Barb.

—*Yes, come on over*—

Jane made yet another pot of coffee and went down the hall to let Barb in. She was pretty in a no-nonsense way, red-rimmed eyes and all. Her blonde hair reminded Jane of George's attempt to disguise himself, keep himself safe.

"Come in, sweetie," Jane said, holding the door open. "You okay?" Finally, it occurred to Jane that Barb loved George, that his being shot and left for dead by an evil monster, was not something Barb was handling very well. "Coffee?"

"Sure," Barb said. When they got into the light streaming into the windows, Jane saw Barb's nose was red, too.

"I haven't known George very long," Jane said,

setting out the vanilla coconut creamer she loved. "But I really like him, and I'm so glad he's okay."

Barb nodded as she put sugar in her coffee, then creamer, then more sugar. "Me, too."

"Let's sit in the sunroom," Jane said. She thought of the times she and George had sat in this same room, across from each other. George with bourbon or at least bourbon in his coffee. "He loved bourbon."

"I didn't know that," Barb said. "Thank Jesus he'll live to drink another day."

They both laughed but not for long. More like a period at the end of a sentence.

"How much sleep did you get?" Barb said.

"Probably more than you did. How's George doing now?"

"He's hanging in there. Regained consciousness. Benton's with him."

"Oh." Jane didn't understand why Barb wasn't there.

"I want to have a family," Barb said. Apparently, talking about personal stuff was all Barb could say at this time. Fine. Jane nodded, hoping Barb would continue.

She did. "I've always wanted to have a family. But when I was younger, I thought I had more time."

"You want to have a family—with George?"

Barb nodded. "He loves me. I didn't know it, not really. He said it to me, but I wasn't sure he was genuine. I mean, he's an actor. Maybe he was acting."

"He wasn't acting. He's crazy about you. You are all he ever talks about."

"Oh." Barb's eyes welled, and she shook her head so the tears flew sideways and not down her cheeks.

"He told me you kissed him. I think that means you have feelings for him, too."

"He told you that, huh?" Barb said. She was laughing and crying, too.

"Yes. He also said an agent is not supposed to fraternize with a CI."

Barb nodded but didn't say anything. Probably some FBI protocol about that.

Barb looked at the romance novel on the table between them, the splayed cover of the paperback's gold lettering catching the light. "You and George. A couple of romantics!"

Jane smiled, happy she kept her grief book on her nightstand. Barb thought she was a romantic! All the weight of yesterday fell away. "I'm really the opposite. But I like seeing it in other people."

Barb studied her. "You're a widow, right?"

"Yes. I didn't have a good marriage. Stayed for the kids. He was a cold bastard. Not to our kids, just to me."

Barb drank her coffee, still looking at Jane over the edge of her cup.

"You know what?" Jane said. "My doctor back in Michigan gave me these anti-anxiety pills when my husband died. I never took one, but last night I finally did and I think they have some kind of truth serum effect, because I don't usually tell people that."

"Don't worry. My middle name is discreet. I just...I always wondered about people like you. The ones who stay in unhappy marriages for the kids. I don't get it."

"Well, I guess, for me, I just had an idea of what kind of life I wanted to give my children. Divorce was not part of the picture."

"But how could you stand it?"

Jane shrugged. She didn't know how she'd done it. "He worked a lot. All the time. Seven days, twelve hours, often more. After the kids went off to college, I caught a little bit of that workaholic thing, started travelling for work. We saw as little as possible of each other."

"I guess I understand how you can do that, trade one important thing for another. I did that at my job. Life is like that. Hard choices. One after the other."

"I don't know. I'm at peace." As Jane said it, she felt something not quite right nagging at her. What was it? Everything was okay. For now. Wasn't it? She sat for a few minutes, waiting to remember the thing she was forgetting. Then she did.

"Oh my God. Barb! Two guys have been hanging out in 205, that's the corner unit. It's usually empty this time of year." Jane pointed away from her and George's condos. "This might be nothing, but our handyman and one of his buddies called them mobsters."

Barb was quiet for a beat. Then she said, "I'm not able to discuss that with you as it concerns an ongoing investigation." She suddenly looked all buttoned up, even though she had a T-shirt on with no buttons at all. Then Barb's phone rang, and Jane went down the hall into her bedroom to give Barb privacy. A few minutes later, Barb called down the hall that she was taking off.

Jane walked to meet her.

"Was that about George? Is he okay?"

"Yes. He's out of ICU. You may come by the hospital and see him later, if you like."

Jane thought about her thing with Jesse. What time

was that supposed to be?

Chapter Fifteen

Jesse picked Jane up at noon. She ran down and got into his spotless unmarked car. She noticed there were only two sharpened pencils in his cup holder today. She had a question she figured he wouldn't answer, but she asked it anyway.

"Did you find out who tossed that braid into my purse at coffee? Does it have anything to do with who killed Waylon?"

Jesse's capable hands stayed steady on the wheel as he for once answered her question. "We've got some information on that. The braid must have been bought online. Nobody bought one like it in any retail outlet within a hundred-mile radius."

"I thought with Halloween not so long ago, maybe it was from a costume shop," Jane said.

Jesse drove with his eyes on the road, even when he spoke, which made Jane feel safe. "We sent it in for DNA testing," he said. "It's not like on television." He stopped at a light and turned to smile at her. "It takes time to get results."

Jane nodded. Florida had very long red lights. Jesse still had his eyes locked on hers. She took a chance. "So you didn't get any DNA from Waylon's bloody shirt yet?"

"No, but it will be soon."

"How soon?"

"Within the next few days. There were complications, which I will explain to you after we've made an arrest."

Jane's heart picked up speed. She wasn't sure if it was because, after ten long days, the killer would finally be caught or because she was alone with Jesse in his car. The scent of his aftershave filled the small space, something musky with lime and fresh cut evergreen branches.

The light turned green, and Jesse focused on the road ahead.

They turned into a subdivision while her thoughts ran away with her. The houses in St. Pete were old; the condos were new. The homes in this neighborhood were mostly tidy brick bungalows, some were a bit more sprawling. The landscaping was lush, full of mature, beautifully cared-for flowering shrubs and majestic royal palms. A sign at the entry proclaimed this part of town a historic district. The streets were cobblestone. A few blocks in, Jesse parked in front of a house that still had Halloween decorations all over the large yard.

"Why are we stopping here?" Jane asked.

"This is the house," Jesse said.

Jane looked at the yard. "You're kidding me, right?"

"Nope." Jesse's smile this time was a full-on grin.

"Poor George," Jane said. How could George have gotten this "clue" so wrong? "He's out of ICU. I met Barb, his FBI handler, this morning."

"Glad he's gonna be okay," Jesse said. "He's a good soldier."

"He'd do anything for Barb."

They studied the lawn in silence for a minute.

"He means well," Jane finally said. "Not sure why he thought fake tombstones and sheets with pumpkin heads on top are art?"

She said it like a question. They couldn't stop themselves; they both laughed a little. It felt good to laugh with Jesse again.

"Apparently so. We talked to the owner. They have four teenagers. The kids love decorating the yard and hate taking it all down. Nobody in the family knows anything about glass beading or copper sculpture or anything else related to Waylon's work."

"Why'd you bring me here, Jesse?"

"Just being thorough." He paused as if debating what he'd say next.

Jesse had not needed to take her for this drive. She felt certain he was interested in getting to know her as a person. Using his job as a pretext to do that, and maybe even unaware that was what he was doing, but happy shivers still danced up and down her spine. She hoped she could trust her feelings.

"You confirmed my theory that George got this one wrong," Jesse finally said. "It's the oldest son who works with George. He doesn't give a fart for art."

Jane, startled, laughed. She recognized the line from a famous poem every art major liked to quote.

"You like poetry?"

"Yes, well, don't let this get around, but I had a literature class forever ago, and I've never forgotten that line. Can't remember the name of the poem, though."

Jane supplied the title, then felt a little embarrassed for showing off.

"I don't want to give you the impression I've got a shelf of poetry books at home," Jesse said. "Mostly I read police reports and once in a while a political biography."

Jane had no idea how to respond to that. Jesse knew she read detective fiction. He had no idea she was also reading a romance novel and a book on complicated grief. Or that, most of the time, she liked to have a non-fiction book going at the same time as her lighter reading material.

He focused on pulling away from the house and heading back to the main roadway. Jane thought about the million things she wanted to ask Jesse. Some were related to the case, and some were not. For a minute there, hiding behind her car during a shoot-out, she had wondered if the bullets were intended for her. She had wanted, in those moments, to live, to experience more than the narrow boundaries her life had thus far shown her. But for today, she'd focus on what she could find out about the investigation.

"So the escaped convict was after George, but he didn't kill Waylon?"

"Correct. The cases remain unrelated. Donaldsin, the convict, was still in prison when Waylon died. And Waylon was not shot."

"So the murder weapon wasn't a gun. Was it one of those fence posts?"

"No," Jesse replied. "Jane, I really can't say any more. But we are going to keep you safe. Patrice is coming over to sit with you today."

"I was going to visit George."

"We can do that now."

"I don't need…" She stopped. If Jesse thought she

needed Patrice as a bodyguard, after last night, she'd go along with it. "I mean, thank you. It's so weird, first George has the FBI living next door, now Patrice is moving in with me? And maybe some kind of gangsters are staying in 205. I'm officially freaking out."

"Hey, you're fine. There are no mobsters in 205. The men who were in 205 yesterday are the good guys. Okay?"

"Yes, okay, but who put the bloody shirt in George's car? George had that theory it was the criminals he pissed off in Detroit."

"We have not found any evidence to support that."

Jane admitted, if only to herself, that she was afraid.

"It's Pip, isn't it?"

"No, we've ruled him out. Patrice got the search warrant for his home, and he had several bags of beads, but he openly admitted they were Waylon's and he swore Waylon had given the beads to him as a gift."

Jane doubted that.

"We can't prove otherwise, and anyway the investigation is leading in another direction."

Jane was really nervous now. She had to bite back a little scream.

"I'm sorry, maybe I shouldn't have told you that. But you are absolutely safe with us, and I thought you should know that the case is coming to a close."

"I'm glad you told me," Jane said. "True, I'm really scared. There's a killer on the loose. He could be anybody. Did the guy who put the braid in my purse, well, was he Randy, my neighbor?"

"Not Randy. But we're being cautious."

They were pulling into a hospital parking lot. Jesse

parked. He walked with Jane up to George's room.

Barb was there. George was awake. They were holding hands.

"Hey, buddy," Jane said. She gave George a motherly kiss on the cheek. "Hi, Barb."

Barb said hello, then to George, "I'm just stepping out to get a bag of chips. You want anything?"

"All I can eat is soup," George said. "Guess I'll have to live on love."

Jane took the seat Barb had vacated.

"Tell me everything."

"She's quitting the Bureau. For me. For us. She had the chance to turn Donaldsin, like she turned me. But she passed the job over to Tom Benton. Her boss was so pissed. She's going to go back to Detroit to close out her employment. There are some details. She may be needed until this case closes. But they'll have to contact her here, because when I get out of this place, she's coming back to Winding Bayou and me."

"I'm so happy for you, George."

"Thanks." He closed his eyes, but he didn't look to be in much pain. Probably had some strong meds in his IV.

"I guess this means you're safe. If Barb's leaving."

"For now. They don't think I'm in immediate danger. Donaldsin has been singing his greatest hits for Benton, and once the round-up of criminals begins, the bosses will know Donaldsin not only failed to kill me, which was meant as a kind of message, keeps the other guys in line, but he's going to be the star witness who puts a bunch of really bad guys in prison. Now all that mess will follow him, not me. I am officially out of it. I don't matter that much to them. But Barb is FBI, as far as they know, and they are not going to fuck with her. Too much heat."

Jane looked back at Jesse, standing near the door. Barb walked back in the room with her bag of chips. Jane got up from the seat, noticing that George was snoring.

"He gave me the scoop," Jane told Barb. "Welcome to the neighborhood!"

"Yeah, it's sweet. I'm going to close up shop in Detroit and be back here before George is released from the hospital."

"So are you both, really, like, safe?"

"Yes. All is well. We managed to elbow George into a safe zone."

"Your arms."

"Pretty much," Barb said. "Details to be worked out with my very pissed-off superiors, but I'm confident we're good. More than."

George snored again, and Jane snickered quietly before she and Jesse said goodbye to Barb.

Chapter Sixteen

Jane was quiet as Jesse drove her home, digesting everything that had happened in the last twenty-four hours. He didn't say much either but followed her upstairs. "I'm staying here until Patrice arrives," he said, getting comfortable on the living room sofa.

Jane felt a tiny shiver. She wasn't sure if it was fear of the killer being revealed or excitement about Jesse being so protective. Her phone pinged. Kim.

—*Okay if I come up?*— Kim's text read.

Jane read the text to Jesse, who was checked his own phone, maybe to see if the DNA evidence had come back from the lab.

"Have her come up," he said. "It's fine."

"You know who killed Waylon," Jane said. It wasn't a question.

"Waiting on DNA evidence."

"It must be someone in Winding Bayou. It's not Pip. It's not the Detroit mob."

Kim rang the bell.

Jesse had made Jane lock her door when they came in, so she went down the hall, Jesse right behind her. Jane let Kim in. Then Jesse locked the door again. Jane and Kim both looked at Jesse.

"What is going on? Did the convict escape?" Kim asked as they made their way into the living room.

"No," Jesse said. "He's in the custody of federal

agents."

"So, why are you staying here until Patrice comes? And why is Patrice coming to babysit me?" Jane plopped down on the chair closest to Jesse.

"Say what?" Kim said, her mouth hanging open after she stopped talking.

Jesse didn't respond right away, so Jane focused on Kim. "Something's going down, and I'm really glad you're here. Did you sleep?"

"Yes."

"How long did Rich stay at your place?"

"Oh, he didn't even come in the door. I was beat. Sent him home. Then I was out like a light. How about you? And how's George?"

"George is going to be okay. I'm fine. Just want Jesse to tell me what the hell is going on."

"I've told you too much already," Jesse said.

"I'm so glad George is okay, and I want to know what's going on, too," Kim said.

Jesse's phone pinged. He looked at it. "I'll let Patrice in," he said, getting up and walking down the hall.

"What's happening, Jane?" Kim wanted to know.

"I'm not sure. I think they know who killed Waylon. Jesse said they didn't get the DNA back yet, but the guys in 205 yesterday were law enforcement."

"FBI?" Kim asked.

Jane shook her head. "I get the feeling they were St. Pete PD."

Patrice came into the living room. Kim and Jane felt comforted that Patrice was on duty once again. She'd protected them from a crazy criminal last night. She would protect them from whatever would happen next.

"Jesse wants to see you at the door," Patrice said to Jane, taking a seat on the sofa.

Jane's fingers and toes tingled. Jesse wanted to see her? He hadn't just left without saying goodbye as usual? She got up and went down the hall to where he stood, a shaft of sunlight falling on his handsome profile.

He reached out and took one of her hands in his, gave it a squeeze. "Are you going to be okay?"

"Yes, of course. I trust Patrice. I'm just nervous, but I'm glad to know this is almost over."

"Okay, good. We have a few open lines of inquiry, and things could happen fast. Or slow. Depends on several variables." He didn't take his eyes off her. "I wish I could say more, and I will, but for now, rest easy. Everything will work out." He had not let go of her hand.

"I'm very happy about that. It's been a tense time."

"For all of us. I've been in business mode, and I know I can be…"

"Abrupt? Distracted?" Jane smiled when she said it.

"Yes." He squeezed her hand, not too tight, and then let go. "But I like you, Jane, and I hope the end of this case is just the beginning of us."

"I hope that, too," she said. A big part of her felt like this was all a dream, and she'd wake up soon in her same old lonely life.

"Lock that door behind me, and do not let anyone in."

"I promise," Jane said. She wanted to kiss him, so she shut the door before she could act on her impulse.

There was all the time in the world to get to know Jesse. She floated back into the living room, where Kim was talking to Patrice.

"I don't get it. Unit 205 is empty. The doctor who owns it never comes here. He rents it out in tourist season. Why would the police go in there?" Kim's words snapped Jane out of her Jesse thoughts.

"Well?" Kim's loud question was aimed at Patrice.

Patrice replied with crazy-making calm, "Not at liberty to say. Ongoing investigation."

"Jesse said Randy was not the person who sent me the braid," Jane said. "Can you at least tell us who did that?"

"We have a suspect," Patrice said.

"Why can't you tell us what the police were doing in 205? According to Jesse, this whole thing is going down soon. Like today. What's the harm of at least telling us who you suspect?" Jane said.

Patrice let out a big sigh. Jane knew between her and Kim, they'd worn the officer down. Good.

"We received a tip. I can't say from who, so don't ask. We think we have the murder weapon. We're waiting on the arrest warrant. That's all I can tell you now."

The murder weapon—Jesse hadn't told her that!

"What? You can't tell us if it was one of our neighbors who killed Waylon?" Kim said.

Patrice looked pained. "Not at this time."

"I do not like the sound of this," Kim said. "Fred has access to every condo key in Winding Bayou. It has to be him."

Jane had suspected Fred, too. But he seemed so sweet. Affable. And he always changed her lightbulbs,

Kim said. Could he really be a murderer?

Patrice didn't say yes or no about Fred. She didn't say anything. Neither did Jane. She was more confused than afraid. Why would Fred kill Waylon?

Patrice remained silent.

"Patrice, is Fred your suspect?" Jane asked.

"Are all your windows secured?" Patrice asked, not answering Jane's question.

"Please tell us," Jane pleaded, but Patrice stayed silent, walking through the sunroom, then the kitchen, checking that the windows were locked.

"I live on the second floor," Jane said. "The weather's been nice. I don't always lock every window!"

Patrice nodded in a friendly way before she headed toward the bedrooms which faced the back of the condos.

Kim got a text and started tapping out a reply with her index finger.

"Rich is coming up," Kim said. "Maybe he knows something."

"Listen," Jane said, "you don't think Fred would bust through my bedroom window, do you?"

"He doesn't seem dangerous at all."

"I know."

"But that's what people always say on television," Kim said. "You have to watch out for the ones who seem like normal guys."

They heard a light tap on the door, not the bell. Or maybe it was Patrice snapping a stray window lock in place.

Kim got up to check the door, and Jane walked into the hall with her. Kim went left toward the door, and

Jane turned right down the bedroom hallway, looking for Patrice. They almost collided in front of the guest room. Patrice quickly moved Jane aside and walked slowly and quietly toward the entry hall.

"It's just Rich," Jane said. She almost ran into Patrice, who had stopped at the mermaid mural and was gesturing with one hand behind her back for Jane to keep out of sight. Patrice's other hand was going for her gun.

"Hey, Rich," Kim said as she opened the door. Jane couldn't see anything because Patrice was blocking her. Why? But Jane stayed. She liked Patrice, and they had been giving her a hard time.

"Where's that bitch, Jane?" Rich said.

Why was everyone down here calling her a bitch all the time? Well, two people. Once each. But still. Rich was saying something Jane didn't catch. Then Kim yelled at him.

"What are you doing?" Kim said. "I know you're happy to see me, but have we not gone over the No Hugging rule before?" Kim said the "no hugging" part in caps. Rich wasn't saying anything now.

And what was Patrice doing with her weapon?

Patrice moved a little away so Jane was able to peek around the corner to see what the hell was happening at the front door. Rich held Kim in a tight hug and swung her around so he was fully inside the condo. He dropped one hand from Kim but kept a firm hold on her with the other.

"I'm sorry, honey," Rich said. "I just want Jane. I don't want to hurt you."

"Then let me go!"

"Hands up, Starling!" Patrice said. Rich paid

neither woman any mind but reached under his belt and pulled a wicked knife from inside his cargo shorts. Jane dropped back out of view.

"I don't want to hurt you, Kim. It's Jane I want to hurt. Jane! Get out here if you care about Kim," Rich yelled.

"Jane! Stay where you are. The situation is under control," Patrice said.

Jane didn't know what to do. She wanted to run out there and save Kim, but Patrice was a police officer and she knew better than anyone how to handle a lunatic. Because that's what it seemed to be…Rich had gone crazy. Crazy…Rich was crazy about Kim. He was not going to pull a knife on her. A knife. That was the murder weapon. And her tires had been cut with a knife, too. Plus, Rich seemed to suddenly be holding a grudge against her. Or maybe he had been, all along, ever since the day he'd met her and she'd swept Kim away to Waylon's house.

"Hands up, I said." Patrice's spine straightened while her knees flexed ever so slightly. Her firing stance, Jane guessed. "Drop the knife, and release the woman!" Patrice's command must have gone unanswered as she gripped her gun in both her hands, aiming toward Jane's front door.

He must be holding Kim and threatening her in some way with the knife. Jane hoped it was not at Kim's throat. Rich wouldn't hurt Kim, would he? Patrice obviously thought so. Jane had to do something. Now. She flattened her back against the wall to the living room. The only wall that was not visible from the front door. She inched her way toward the living room and her phone.

"Where's Jane?" Rich yelled.

She pressed herself against the wall and carefully slid against it into the living room. She grabbed her phone from its cradle on the end table and texted one word to Jesse. Her fingers were slick with sweat as she spelled out

—*Trouble!*—

She wiped her hands on her shorts, taking deep breaths to calm herself and block out everything except pressing 911.

"911. What's your emergency?"

Jane wished she could scream to vent her taut nerves, but instead she whispered, "An armed man is in my house. He doesn't know I'm here."

"Okay. What's your name?"

"Jane Chasen."

"Where are you in the home in relation to the intruder?"

Jane fought panic and annoyance. "He's in the hallway. I'm in the living room. Can you please just come and get him? Last I saw, he had a very nasty knife on my friend's throat."

"Is there somewhere you can hide?"

"I'll find somewhere. But my friend…"

"We have your location and a unit is being sent. Please stay on the phone with me until help arrives, Jane."

"Okay, fine, but I don't want him to hear me."

"You're doing so well, Jane. You don't have to say another word unless you feel it's necessary. For now, find a place to hide."

Just then, Patrice said, "Jane's in the bathroom," and then added, "The one in her bedroom."

The operator asked, "Is there another person with you?"

Patrice must had sensed Jane going into the living room, not the bedroom. She wasn't sure why Patrice wanted Rich in the master bathroom. She must be buying time. Patrice had to know Jane would call Jesse. Didn't she always call him when the trouble started?

"Yes," Jane whispered. "A police officer. She has a gun on the intruder. She's directing him away from me."

She looked around for a place to hide. Bookshelf. Cabinet. Television. Sofa. Chairs. Sunroom. More chairs. Her antique bar cart. That might work. She tried to move as quickly and silently as possible. She had no weapon, but she could throw martini glasses if necessary.

She didn't convey any of this to the 911 operator. She was too afraid Rich would hear her and hurt Kim. Or maybe she should yell something to distract Rich so Patrice could take him down? She put her phone on the bar cart and grabbed a martini glass in each hand.

Where was Jesse?

"Stop!" Patrice yelled. "Let Kim go. You don't want to hurt her."

"I don't. You're right. That's why we're all going in the bedroom to get Jane," Rich said. "Then I'll let Kim go. I don't want to hurt her, but if I have to, I will."

Patrice was saying something in a soothing voice to Rich, Rich's flip-flops slapped the ceramic tiles as he walked down the hall, coming farther into the condo. What kind of criminal takes hostages in flip-flops? Jane hoped Rich had been stupid and left the front door open, too. From the calming murmur of Patrice's voice, Jane knew they were in her bedroom. Rich had not spotted her behind the bar cart, but any second now, he would know Patrice had lied and Jane was not in the master bath.

Then what would happen? She pictured storming in with martini glasses, but Patrice might shoot her by mistake.

After this was over, if she was still alive, Jane vowed to buy her own firearm and take shooting lessons twice a week until she could hit a target in the head or the heart or wherever it would do the most damage. She was going to keep her weapon close at all times. Maybe even sleep with it under her pillow.

A gun went off, and Jane startled, dropping one of the martini glasses. She put the other one on the cart and picked up her phone.

The operator said, "Jane? Are you okay? Did I hear a weapon fire?"

Rich yelled and cursed nonstop so Jane said, "I think the officer shot him."

Jane's ears were ringing, then Jesse came in, and as he started to approach her, she pointed down the hall toward her bedroom. Weapon out, he joined the fray.

"Another officer has arrived. Thank you." Jane clicked off the phone and slumped on the floor beside the broken martini glass.

Chapter Seventeen

Two cop cars pulled in downstairs, sirens blaring. "Patrice, your friends are here," Jane said, easing off the floor next to the bar cart and broken glass. Patrice walked a handcuffed Rich from the bedroom, followed by Kim and Jesse. Jane was going to have to do a sage smudging ceremony to get rid of Rich's evil energy. Four uniformed cops came into the hallway, and Patrice handed Rich over to them. Rich was led outside. He was limping and left a trail of blood. Kim almost collapsed into Jane's arms. Jane led Kim to the living room and gently sat her down.

"Does everyone want water?"

"Thanks, Jane," Patrice said, pulling out her notebook and handing Jesse a pencil. He had a little notebook, too. Jane guessed they compared notes. Literally. Patrice better get a promotion after this!

Jane filled a pitcher with water and arranged it with four glasses on a tray.

"Should I make coffee?" Jane asked as she set the tray down. Her hands were remarkably steady.

"No, we won't stay long," Jesse said. "After we go over what's been happening here, you two can come down to the station to make an official statement."

Jane and Kim both said okay. Kim's voice was strong, Jane noted.

"It was Rich?" Kim asked, after taking a sip of the

water Jane handed her. "All this time? He was jealous of Waylon." She sniffed. "I'm glad I jabbed my knee into his nuts."

"That was a brave move. You managed to make him drop the knife, and I was able to shoot him in the foot once you moved out of range," Patrice said.

Jesse started writing. Jane loved that he was such a careful note-taker. There was something so endearing about it. Either that or she was smitten.

"Was that murder weapon you found in 205 a butcher knife?" Kim asked. "You all know he was a butcher back in Texas before he retired?"

"We did," Patrice said. "We have been watching the owners on the first floor since Jane told Jesse about the work-around they had with the busted security camera and the first-floor front doors. We combed over their information more than once. Waylon had been murdered with a professional-grade meat-carving knife. We put those two things together pretty quickly, and we got a warrant, but the knife was not in Rich's condo."

The persistent image Jane had of Waylon being stabbed came back to her.

Goosebumps prickled on her arms. Someone had slashed the tires of her car with a knife. "Did Rich slash the tires on my car? Why does he want to hurt me?"

"He did slash your tires," Jesse said.

"But why? It doesn't make sense. I've never done anything to him. And then he came and picked us up after the convict was captured."

"He wanted to be a hero. And you did do something to him, in his mind anyway. You introduced me to Waylon," Kim added. "Plus he was jealous of Waylon because I cared about him and because Waylon was an artist, which is so much sexier than being a butcher. Don't you think?"

"I do," Jane said. "Indeed I do."

"Rich was jealous of Waylon's creativity, and you're the one who made people start looking at Waylon differently, Jane."

Jane began to understand why a murderer could hold a grudge against her.

"But what about the bloody shirt?" Jane asked. "Why would Rich put the shirt in George's car? It makes no sense."

"Did you forget that George put suntan lotion on my shoulders?" Kim said. "I thought it would be good for Rich to see that. He wouldn't stop trying to romance me, even though I was not feeling it. He had such a weird way of showing his emotions. He—it's complicated. Like, I didn't think he was jealous. He never acted that way. I don't know. He's weird."

Sirens blared again with their loopy woop-woo. Rich was on his way to jail. It was finally over. Waylon Silvercloud's murderer had been apprehended. They were safe. Jane almost fainted when she remembered that just last night, Rich had driven her home from the other shoot-out. She'd been in a murderer's car. Waylon's murderer.

"Wait! Are you sure Rich slashed my tires?"

"Yes," Jesse said. "We found the knife he used for that, and our own guys were able to quickly get a match."

Jane could breathe again.

"But how?" Jane was puzzled. "How would he be a hero?" The whole knife thing made her shudder.

"I know that one," Kim said. "He wanted to get

lucky. He wanted to rescue us, and he wanted me to be so grateful I'd fool around with him. Right? But Rich wouldn't know there'd be a shoot-out happening at the same time. Just dumb luck. Emphasis on dumb."

Everybody's phone pinged. Jane retrieved her phone from under the sofa pillow and read the Winding Bayou notification. People should feel free to go about their business. The murderer had been captured and taken downtown to jail. The judge was said to be tough on violent crime and was not likely to let him out on bail. Winding Bayou was a safe community once again.

"So, I still don't get it." Jane's head hurt from holding so many questions. "There was no knife in Rich's condo. Did he kill Waylon with something else? What was it?"

"A knife was our murder weapon. And we found it in 205," Jesse said.

"But how? Was Fred in on it?" Kim asked.

"We've been talking to Fred since Jane found the braid in her purse."

"Technically, I found it," Kim said.

"You did," Jane affirmed. She asked Kim if she wanted anything.

"No, just water."

Jane got up and handed Kim the glass of water that had been sitting on the table next to her. Kim sipped.

"You're so brave. Where was the knife? I kept picturing it across your throat!" Jane said.

"Well, that's right." Kim rubbed her neck. "What a gosh-damn creep."

"So how did you move to kick him without getting your throat slashed?" Jane asked.

Kim took a long sip of water, and she asked Patrice

to help her demonstrate for Jesse's notes.

"You sure you're up to it?" Patrice asked, standing next to Kim, pretending to hold a knife to her throat.

"Well, I'm not going to kiss you!" Kim said. "But that's what I did with Rich. He was always wanting to kiss on me. So I leaned into him kinda hard and turned an inch or so like this"—Kim's mouth was close to Patrice's—"and then he loosened the knife to kiss me back, so I turned quick and jammed my knee in his privates, and Patrice shot him at the same time. He went down like a ton of dog doo."

"He was howling," Patrice confirmed.

"And he had lost the knife. Patrice kicked it under your bed, Jane."

"Thanks for reminding me. Shall I bag the knife, Jesse?" Patrice asked.

"Wait and let crime scene do it," he said.

"So Rich was holding his crotch, like that would do any good, and he was crying and saying how could I hurt him, he loved me."

"When exactly during this dance did Patrice shoot Rich?" Jesse asked.

"Well, I noticed that Kim was trying to distract Rich, and it was working. The knife had slid away from her neck, and he wasn't paying a bit of attention to me, so I shot him in the foot maybe a second before Kim kneed him in the balls, er, scrotum."

"I'm not sure which one of us hurt him the most!" Kim said. Patrice and Kim slapped a high five, then Patrice glanced at Jesse and wiped the victory smile off her face.

"He was clearly incapacitated, and I was able to subdue and cuff him. At which point, you came into the scene," Patrice told Jesse.

Jane had not been at the "scene" yet. The crime lab people came in the door just then, and Jesse showed them into Jane's bedroom. She was a little bit sad that his first impression of her most private space was marred by crime. His first look at her bed would be to point out where the knife was located.

She would go on Pinterest later for ideas on colors that looked good with ocean-blue walls. She'd choose new sheets, new lightweight blanket, new duvet, new pillow shams, all of it. Meanwhile, she'd sleep in the guest room. Nobody had stayed in it yet, but she had a little portable crib for Suzy in the closet and the queen bed had a brand-new mattress. She loved the light sea-green color of the walls. She'd be fine in there until after the smudging ceremony.

"Oh, what?" Jane realized that Patrice was telling a story about unit 205. "I'm sorry, I didn't hear that first part."

"We questioned Fred, since, as Kim pointed out, he had keys to every unit. When he realized he could be arrested as an accomplice, along with Rich, he opened up the vault. Apparently, Rich asked Fred to let him in 205 the morning after Waylon died. Fred didn't think anything of it. Rich was his buddy, not a murderer. Rich told Fred he was out of whiskey and what with the Indian killing he needed a snort and his pension check wasn't coming for another week. Fred had told Rich about the fine liquor cabinet he'd seen on a previous occasion when he'd had to let in pest control. So Fred let Rich in and agreed to stand outside as a lookout in case anybody came by."

"Fred's a nice guy, but he's stupid. He's gonna get

fired for this, because it was wrong to let Rich in there. And if he'd fixed the security camera in the parking lot, we'd have figured out Rich killed Waylon a long time ago." Kim fumed at the stupidity of her most steadfast admirer. Or that's how Jane read her friend's face. Between Fred and Rich, there was surely enough stupid to go around.

"But what about when they told me those men I saw carrying grocery bags were mobsters?" Jane said.

"Fred swore they were just teasing you, Jane. He and Rich figured they were FBI same as that other fella."

Jane's thoughts were spinning. "And Rich didn't get nervous about his knife being in 205?"

"No," Patrice said. "The whole FBI thing was an excellent distraction. Fooled both Rich and Fred."

"They were fools already," Kim said. To Jane's ears, she still sounded huffy, and she had every right to be pissed. Rich was way worse than Stan had ever been.

"Do we know why Rich put the bloody shirt into George's car?"

"Oh hell, I can answer that one, too. Jane already knows this," Kim said. "He didn't like that George put suntan lotion on my shoulders! Told me so one time! Nerve of that guy."

"Thanks for that tip, Kim. You two have been great with filling in the blanks," Jesse said.

"So, ready with the notebooks? I'm going to explain how the convict case and Waylon's murder are related." Jane's mystery-reading mind had finally sewn up that last unruly thread.

Jesse made a show of whipping his notebook out and licking his pencil.

"Okay, ready," he said. He was grinning, and so was Patrice. Jane figured they knew what was coming.

"*Your* undercover officers were pretending to be FBI agents. Without George being hunted by a criminal and the FBI coming in to help him lay a trap, Rich would have totally been suspicious about those guys in 205. He could have left town. Disappeared," Jane proclaimed.

Jesse chuckled. "Well, you're not wrong, Jane. The FBI helped our case. Helped us catch a killer."

"I knew it!" Jane said.

"So the motive was jealousy?" Jesse asked Kim. "Rich had feelings for you?"

She nodded. "I guess you could say that. But I didn't return his sentiments, I can assure you."

"And what about the braid?" Jane wanted to know.

"It's like Kim said. We think Rich was upset because you made a big deal over Waylon," Patrice said. "He maybe wanted to put you in your place. Scare you a little."

"I've got to leave soon, as that is one of the many questions I have for Rich." Jesse looked at Jane.

She remembered what he said about wanting to get to know her better after the case was over. She winked at him, then she added to the murder story. "I talked Kim into coming down to Waylon's with me. From the minute they set eyes on each other, it was true love. Rich must have guessed that. He'd wanted to come down to Waylon's with us, but we ditched him at the clubhouse."

"I'm sorry for your loss, Kim," Patrice said.

"I know. You all told me," Kim said. "It doesn't really help, but I'll get over it in time."

"It's all so sad," Jane said. "Sad for you, and Waylon's family and friends. I'm so glad you guys caught his killer."

"With a little help from you two," Patrice said. Jesse didn't deny it.

"Okay, ladies, I think we have everything." Jesse stood. "Since Rich was never in this part of the condo, you can stay here while the lab folks finish up. They won't be too much longer."

"Can we come to the station tomorrow to give our statements?" Kim asked. "I'm so out of sorts, I'm not sure I can walk downstairs again."

"Yes, of course. Tomorrow is fine," Patrice told them. Jesse nodded.

"Thank you both," Jane said.

"Just doing our job," Patrice said.

Jesse came to Jane's chair and put a hand on her shoulder and squeezed, the same way he'd squeezed her hand earlier. She felt her face warm and hoped she was not blushing. Jesse bent down to whisper in her ear. "I'll call you later?" He said it like a question, so Jane nodded okay.

After Jesse and Patrice left, Kim said, "What did he whisper to you?" Then she said, "No, don't tell me yet. You got wine?"

"What do you think?" Jane said. She hustled to change the water into wine.

"He said he'll call me later," Jane admitted, after they'd had a little wine.

"Should I have told the cops about the E.D.? " Kim said.

"What?"

"You know. Where a guy can't get it up, so he has

175

to take pills. Rich told me about it. He couldn't take the pills because he had a heart attack. He had to have special medicine so he didn't go crazy with lust. But it made him crazy anyway when I started seeing Waylon."

"Huh. Getting old sure is complicated."

"You just wait until you're my age," Kim said and cackled.

****

After Kim left, Jane tried to read, but her mind was too busy. She wanted music, but old style. On a record player. She settled for asking Alexa to play "I Want to Know What Love Is" while shopping online. She bought a simple stereo she could just plug in and gifted herself with her top one dozen albums on vinyl. It was close to Christmas, after all. Only a month or so left.

Jane's first memories of music were being at home with Mom, while Dad was at work, listening to Bob Dylan and the Beatles. Both the stories her mom read to her as a child and one of the Dylan songs started with the same words: "Once upon a time." She still listened to Dylan, and her mom still played the same Joni Mitchell albums Jane remembered from those childhood days.

As the song swelled around her, she wondered what Marisol remembered most about her childhood. She shivered even though the temperature outside was warmer than she'd ever known this close to Thanksgiving. Marisol needed time to think things over, like Paul Rogers sang about taking a little time to think things over.

Should she call her kids and tell them what had happened? Jane couldn't decide. She was tired of thinking. She got out her sketchpad and doodled. She drew a portable record player, like the first one she got as a birthday gift as a young girl. Then she drew a human arm reaching for the arm on the old record player. She drew the tiny diamond needle, but she needed a sharper pencil so she tried to remember her favorite album cover. Maybe Carole King's *Tapestry*, with Carole King sitting on a window seat in her bare feet and bell bottoms and peasant blouse. Her curly hair and smiling eyes.

She sat for an hour filling in the page with a tulip-shaped gramophone and an iPod. Did she still have her iPod? Probably not. She'd been going for streamlined when she moved and donated it along with everything else. She drew the eight-track player that sat under the dash of her dad's classic car and the first cassette player she bought to make mix tapes. The page was too full to draw anything else, but at least her mind was finally clear. Maybe she'd go to Queenie's painting class. Everyone said you didn't need to know anything about art or painting. Jane thought she probably knew too much. That might be what had kept her away from class, all her preconceived notions.

She wasn't hungry, so she made popcorn for dinner and turned on the television to see if the local news was reporting on the story. Photos of Rich, one at the beach, one mug shot, soon popped onto the screen. Jane turned up the volume.

"…terror in the Winding Bayou condominium development today as a retired butcher from Texas is charged with first degree murder. The murder weapon? A butcher knife."

Jane stopped chewing and had to go spit out the

popcorn she'd tried to eat. She could eat tomorrow. Tonight, she watched as the community came into focus, in particular, the back end of the visitor parking lot where the dumpsters were kept. The reporter on scene showed the news anchor how the fence had been cut behind the dumpsters. "This is where police say suspect Richard Starling allegedly used a bolt cutter to open the fencing for a fast escape after the gruesome and bloody killing of Waylon Silvercloud, a local artist and activist and member of the Seminole Nation." The reporter didn't touch the fence but used her finger to point to Waylon's back yard.

"Just beyond those trees, Silvercloud was working in his backyard studio. He had apparently been firing art objects in a kiln and had removed his shirt just before Starling entered and began slashing."

The picture switched to a city official, maybe the mayor, reading a prepared statement. "The manner of killing was consistent with the butchering of an animal. Richard Starling allegedly, cold-bloodedly, used the victim's own shirt to wipe blood from himself after he'd killed Silvercloud. There's no question this was a premeditated act. Starling allegedly cut the fence before he entered Silvercloud's yard. He had every intention of killing a man he saw as a romantic rival. If convicted, local government has every intention of prosecuting him to the full extent of the law. And yes, that may mean the death penalty."

The story shifted focus back to the onsite reporter, still at the Bayou's back parking lot. She'd moved away from the gaping fence and stood with her microphone wrapped in both hands. Jane thought she could open her windows and look out and see the reporter. But she didn't.

"Police suspect Starling, who lived in this building"—the camera focused on Rich's unit—"simply dumped the bloody shirt in a neighbor's car. As you can see, these units have garages. One unfortunate neighbor had parked in the visitor's lot close to the dumpsters and, as you see, the fence line bordering the condo development from the outside community street. It is thought Starling had a similar grudge against the man who owned the car. We are not releasing his name at this time, and the Winding Bayou Owner's Association has asked St. Petersburg citizens to respect the privacy of this gated community's residents."

A shot of the front of the complex, including the guard shack, snapped into focus. "Yes, Winding Bayou is a gated community. Although, sadly, we have seen that gates can be easily breached." Now the shot of the gaping fence came into view. "Back to you in the studio, Brad and Erin."

One of the talking heads said thank you to the reporter on scene. They wrapped up the segment with a promise of a "full report" on the victim and a "statement from the Seminole Nation at six p.m."

The male anchor turned to the female. "So. Not a hate crime?"

"No," the female answered. "In this case, it's a twisted love crime, Brad."

The television went to commercial, and Jane turned it off. Maybe she should call Marisol and Danny. If this story went national, and they saw the condo on the news, they'd want to know she was okay. But how likely would it be for the story to spread? Jane googled the story and saw that it was all over the internet. Okay.

It was hours earlier in Seattle. She texted Danny with a link to the story and adding that she was fine. Then she called Marisol.

"Mommy!" Marisol said. She only called Jane "Mommy" when she was feeling vulnerable and upset. "Are you okay?"

Danny texted back a thumbs-up.

"I'm fine, honey." Jane wondered if she should tell Marisol that the murderer had been in her house, holding her best friend hostage in Jane's own bedroom. With a knife. She really didn't want to frighten Marisol, so instead she talked about Waylon, and how she'd met him a few weeks ago, and how talented he was and what a loss to the community his death was.

"But Mom, did you know the St. Pete Butcher?"

"Not very well. He lived in my building. He sat at the same table with me for coffee in the clubhouse, but we weren't friendly." Jane would leave out that she'd been in Rich's car just the night before. It seemed like a lifetime ago. She hadn't even had time to see what the local coverage had been of the shooting at the Boat House.

"It's like the Wild West out there!" Marisol said.

"Detroit has hundreds of homicides a year; this is the first one in St. Pete since I've been here, honey."

Marisol's tone softened. "I'm sorry for what I said about Dad."

Jane only realized she had a headache when she felt the blood pounding in her head. "It's okay, sweetie. I know how much you loved your father."

"But you didn't love him, did you?"

Jane switched the phone into her left hand and massaged her forehead with her right. "In my way, I loved him," Jane said. That was true. She loved the memory of their love. She'd been going back over the early years, the good years. It was part of the complicated grief process. "Every marriage—nobody can really know what goes on in a marriage except the two people in it."

"I guess. You guys just seemed like strangers who happened to live in the same house."

Jane thought of how best to answer her daughter. "We were living our lives, working too much, both of us. Never enough time…"

"Do you think you would have been closer if Daddy didn't work so much?"

"Maybe. The main thing to know is that I loved your father and he loved me. You were very much wanted, Marisol. Danny too."

"Okay, Mom. Did you keep the wedding album?" Marisol had loved to look through the pictures of Jane and Stan's church wedding. Jane in her long dress and veil. Stanley in his tuxedo. They'd been kids.

"Yes. I have it."

"I'm going to come out for Thanksgiving. The three of us are. We can look through the album."

"That would be great, honey. I hope you can get a good price on a flight."

"I already bought the tickets. Last week."

That surprised Jane. And consoled her. "The guest room is ready and waiting."

"Yeah. We're staying with Granny and G-pa. Danny and Julie are going to stay at yours. But we'll visit. I want to look through the album."

Jane's headache lifted. "Probably for the best," she said. It would all come out, she realized. Her level of involvement in this murder. She wondered if she should give the wedding album to Marisol. But no. Her daughter might look at the gesture as evidence that Jane did not care. She had cared. So long ago, but it had been real.

"Why do you say that?" Marisol's tone had gone up a notch.

Jane told her the whole story. "I haven't told Danny that part yet. Or your grandparents. But I will. They're still on their cruise."

"Thanks for telling me, Mom. You need to do a smudge ceremony."

"I know. Sage, right?"

"Yes. Use white sage. And do you have a hand bell? Ring it in the four corners of every room."

"I'll get the bell when I buy sage. There's a health food place here that has supplies." Jane had not been in the health food store, but she'd passed it and read the claims for "healing herbs" many times. She hoped that wasn't just code for medical marijuana.

"I'm looking forward to being in St. Pete. It's so dreary here now."

Seattle wasn't a city of perpetual rain, Jane had found. It rained in winter, but had beautiful springs and summers. She liked to fly west in those months. Florida's hurricane season was a good time to get out of town.

She and Marisol said goodbye. Jane only realized after they'd disconnected that she'd called the old way, no FaceTime.

Chapter Eighteen

Thanksgiving was late this year. Only a few days before December. On Thanksgiving morning, Jane surveyed her new dining room, which had until a few days ago been a blank space outside her galley kitchen. Sometimes empty spaces felt good to her, and she'd had no problem leaving this part of her new home open for several months. But then the kids decided to come in for Thanksgiving, and she almost immediately knew she'd host her first family Thanksgiving in her new home.

She'd chosen the lovely iron chandelier, with its softly scrolling arms, white French linen upholstered chairs, and natural creamy-colored maple dining table, extended today to seat twelve. She'd positioned the high chair she'd bought for Little Suzy at the head of the table. She and Marisol would sit on either side of their girl.

Her phone rang. She answered quickly, hoping it wouldn't wake Danny and Julie.

Jesse. "Are you sure I can't bring anything today?"

"Positive!" Jesse's sons would be spending Thanksgiving with their mother, and if Jane had not invited him, he would have likely gone in to work, as Patrice had told her he often did on holidays, so cops with families could spend special time with them. When Jane had heard that, she decided Jesse had to come to Thanksgiving dinner with her family. And he said yes to her invitation. He'd also hung the chandelier, using tools from her pink toolbox.

"I got a call from Waylon's mom yesterday," Jane told Jesse.

"What's new with the art installation project?"

"The Seminole are building him his own museum. They're doing it just the way we imagined, with the installation outside in a yard-like space and the work studio as part of the main building. They're building an addition that will offer glass-blowing demonstrations using Waylon's signature colors." Jane felt teary-eyed just thinking about it. Waylon was dead, but his legacy lived on.

"That's great news, sweetie."

Jane liked Jesse's nickname for her. She'd denied herself this kind of relationship for too long. Now she welcomed it. She was learning to let love in again.

"So the DNA evidence finally came through?" Now a trial date could be set. At last.

"Yep. This makes everything we already knew official."

"So did Rich confess to planting the braid in my purse?"

"He did. I don't know what he thought would happen by refusing to cooperate. No matter. They found his DNA on George's car, the bloody shirt, the Bayou trash bin, the gloves Rich threw into it, even in the knife drawer in unit 205. For someone who thought he was so smart, he turned out to be remarkably dumb," Jesse said. Then, changing the subject, he asked if the turkey was in the oven.

"Yes. Everything is ticking like clockwork. Kim is

baking a pumpkin pie downstairs, and George is bringing a special bourbon pecan pie. Barb is whipping fresh cream!"

"See. I should bring something."

"You're bringing you, and that's all I care about."

He called her sweetie again when he said goodbye.

Jane and Jesse weren't rushing into anything, but they had gotten to be amazing friends in a short span of time and slowly they were turning it into something more. She had even shown him her sketchbook. She'd not shown another soul her sketchbooks, not in her entire life. Only Jesse. He encouraged her to try Queenie's art class. She hadn't yet, although she signed up for the first January session, when the snowbirds would begin to flock south. Jane reasoned a larger class would help her feel less self-conscious.

"Do I smell coffee?" Danny came out of the guest room in cut off sweatpants and a T-shirt. "Or is that a turkey roasting?"

"Good morning!" Jane smiled so wide her face was in danger of cracking. She had her boy under her roof again, and it felt wonderful. "Coffee's in the pot. Turkey's in the oven."

She walked around her new table to get to the snack bar on the other side of the galley kitchen and watched her son pour a coffee and peek into the oven for a look at the bird. "That's one big fowl," Danny remarked.

"Want some Irish cream in your coffee?"

"Yum. That sounds good."

"It's in the fridge."

Danny opened the fridge and hooted out a laugh. "Boy, does this remind me of home! No room to fit a raisin in here!"

Jane giggled. She'd been cooking and prepping for a week and loved every minute of it. She clicked the remote that raised the shades in the sunroom. Blue sky and brilliant sun. Another day in paradise.

"Honey, watch the parades if you like." Jane pointed out the newspaper on the coffee table. "I know you love to read all the Black Friday sale inserts," she said.

"It's my job," Danny joked, sitting in Jesse's favorite spot on the sofa. He and Julie would be catching a late flight home to Manhattan tonight. Wall Street was wide open the day after Thanksgiving.

Julie came out wearing one of the robes Jane had hung in the guest room, a towel around her hair.

"Coffee?" Jane said.

"Yes, please. Then maybe I can finish getting dressed."

"You kids were up late last night."

"I love when people call me a kid! I'm twenty-eight, Mom Chasen." She smiled when she said it and took the cup of coffee from Jane before heading back down the hall toward the guest room. Jane had gone to the health food store as Marisol suggested. She'd not only found white sage and a Tibetan brass bell, but hired the owner of the store to do a special cleansing ceremony. Patrice and Kim had attended in wide-eyed wonder. Jane was at peace with her home again. And Rich was in jail where he deserved to be.

Jane checked her list while Danny watched the Macy's parade. Time to mash the potatoes. They'd stay hot on the stovetop warmer until dinner. Mom already promised to make her special gravy. Jane had purchased the correct flour Mom insisted was the secret to really good gravy. First, she grabbed a tray of cinnamon rolls from the warmer in the oven and transferred two to a plate and took them into Danny, who despite his fancy digs and big career still had a sweet tooth in the morning.

The phone rang again. Her mom checking in, asking the same question Jesse had asked. "If you make the gravy and Dad carves the turkey, that's all the help I need. My friends here are doing dessert."

"If you're sure…" Mom said.

"I am, but thanks for offering. How'd Suzy sleep?"

"I didn't hear her all night," Mom said. "Thanks for the loan of the portable crib."

"Of course," Jane said.

"Sounds like a parade at your house."

"Danny's watching. Julie's getting dressed. I'm about to mash potatoes. Oh! Tell Dad not to forget his guitar. I've been bragging about him to my friends."

"He says he'll only play during commercials." Danny and Dad loved watching the Lions game on Thanksgiving. Stan had watched it with them, since his business was closed every Thanksgiving. "And not half time!"

"Sounds like a plan."

"Okay then, dear, if you're sure you don't need anything."

"I'm sure." Jane knew her mother would arrive loaded down with wine and chocolates and her famous cashew brittle. And probably something lovely for Jane's home. She knew Jane had ordered roses with fall foliage for the table centerpiece. Maybe a family heirloom, which Mom had been doing a lot in the last several years.

Jane had been at her mom's last week dropping off the portable crib, and she'd noticed the pair of small oil paintings that had always hung in the hallway with other framed family photos had been replaced by the latest photo of Suzy in a frame that complemented Suzy's little rainbow tutu. Maybe Mom had wrapped the old portraits up for Marisol. Jane hoped Marisol would at least pretend to be pleased with the portraits, a boy and a girl dressed in Victorian-era clothing, nobody in their family as far as they knew, in matching burnished gold frames. Jane was an only child, and little by little, her mother had been handing down the family treasures, mostly to Jane, but sometimes to Danny or Marisol.

Danny was a darling son, loving and quiet, but also plainspoken. He always stood his ground and let others deal with whatever they felt about it. He'd been that way since he was a small boy. So when his grandmother had given him the gold cuff links her father had received upon retirement after forty years as an auto executive, Danny had taken them and said, "Thanks, Gran. I don't wear cuff links, but I'll keep these in the drawer next to the tie pin you gave me last year." He'd hugged her and had been obviously pleased with the gift even though it was not useful.

George and Barb were the first to arrive, when Danny was still in his cut-off sweats. Just in time for introductions, Julie came out from the bedroom with her hair half in rollers and told Danny to go change before his grandparents arrived, and he'd hopped off the sofa, kissed her on the cheek, and said, "Yes, dear." Jane's heart almost burst with love and happiness. Love was what this day was all about.

"Where should I put the pie?" Barb asked.

George took it from her and stashed it on top of the fridge. Then he opened the liquor cabinet above the fridge and brought out the bourbon. Jane was already filling his glass with ice, and he poured while thanking her.

Barb rolled her eyes at Jane.

"Prosecco?" Jane asked. She had two different chilled bottles on the countertop, to which George had added the bottle of bourbon.

"Better make it the nonalcohol one." Barb pointed to the sparkling cider.

Hmm, Jane thought. She didn't say anything, just poured.

Kim came next, stowed her pumpkin pie next to the bourbon-pecan one, and took a glass of wine from the tray of flutes Jane assembled. Julie came in from the bedroom looking chic from her dark, shiny pageboy hair down to her impeccable burnt orange toenails. They matched her snug T-shirt that showcased a tiny baby bump. George, immediately after introductions, poured her the nonalcohol version of wine his possibly pregnant new wife was drinking. They hadn't made any announcement yet, although last night Danny had revealed the happy surprise to Jane.

"He'll be born in June, just like Dad."

Jane had wordlessly hugged Danny.

Marisol had kept Suzy's gender under wraps until she was born. Danny could not contain his pride. Jane marveled at the symmetries of life. She'd had a boy and girl and now her grandchildren were a boy and a girl. Although when she'd mentioned it to Marisol, Jane's daughter had responded that she planned another pregnancy when Suzy was two. And Jane was happy. She'd been an only child, and while it had been better than fine, in fact she'd always felt especially beloved, but she'd also thought siblings would be nice, too.

Jesse came in with Jane's folks, still introducing themselves, and sure enough Dad had his guitar in one hand and a larger bag in the other. Her mom had a box of wrapped packages, even though it wasn't Christmas yet. Jesse handed Jane a pricey bottle of chilled champagne. As her parents passed them to greet the family in the living area—they'd not seen Danny and Julie yet—Jesse and Jane lingered a moment by the mermaid mural. He kissed her. It wasn't the first time he'd done that, so it was okay that the kiss was cut short by the ringing doorbell. Jane realized Jesse would have closed the door for a moment of privacy. But he didn't lock it, as Marisol, carrying Suzy—Susan, Jane corrected herself—and Marisol's husband Anwar walked in.

"Stay until everyone clears out?" Jane said in a low tone meant only for him.

"You bet," Jesse answered.

Then Jane hugged Susan as she introduced her daughter to Jesse. Marisol gave Susan to Jane to hold and led the way into the living area. Jane squeezed Susan, not too tightly, and kissed her forehead. Susan knew her well enough from their weekly FaceTime calls to smile and make little sounds that were almost words.

Then Susan fussed to get down, demanding to "Ak, ak" which was possibly baby-speak for walk, so Jane set her on her feet and held one tiny hand while Jesse took the other. The three of them walked in last to the party of family and friends.

****

Later, after every dish was done, after every slice of pie had been consumed, every early gift had been opened and exclaimed over, after Suzy had crashed out on the sofa next to her Uncle Danny, Jane's dad said he'd play a new set.

"Wait until Jane and I return," her mom said, pulling Jane into the kitchen and handing her one of the wrapped gifts she'd arrived with. She'd already privately given Marisol gifts at home, she said, and Jane had noticed her take Danny and Julie into the guest room to bestow whatever present she'd wrapped for them. Jane's mom was the most generous person Jane had ever met.

Jane tore open the tissue carefully and knew what she had as soon as she saw a corner of a burnished gold frame. The Victorian boy and girl. Her mom told the story Jane had heard for many years. "My mother bought these because the children reminded her of my brother and me." Both Grandma and Jane's uncle were dead now. Jane's mom was the oldest alive on her side of the family. The matriarch.

Jane's eyes welled, and she looked up to stop the tears from falling. Her mom had taught her that trick, so she knew what Jane was doing. Jane blinked away the happy tears and hugged her mom. "Thank you, Mommy," she said. It occurred to her right then that Marisol had probably heard Jane call her mother "Mommy" at emotional times, and that's what Marisol did now with Jane. One of so many family traditions.

"I think they look a bit like Marisol and Danny,

don't you?"

And Jane looked again at the portraits. She agreed.

"If you don't have a place for them, you can put them away…"

"I think they'd look nice in the dining room." The dining room opened into the living room and galley kitchen, the other wall had two large closets, and the one large blank wall. Jane hadn't hung anything on it yet.

"I did notice that the gold on the frames harmonizes nicely with the wood on the chairs." Mom said.

They took the art out to the dining room, and Marisol looked over with interest. Jane guessed she'd been in on the surprise.

"I'll have to think about where I want these." Jane held them up to the big wall. Too small for that much wall, but she could add some other art. Maybe. Then there was the small wall between the two closets. Jane placed them vertically. Maybe. The final spot was the wall between the kitchen and sunroom. She walked over and placed them there. Jesse came to stand beside her and her mom.

"They look perfect there, don't they?"

Marisol joined to give her opinion and perhaps to sniff out the relationship between her mother and the police detective. Kim came over just then, and Jane felt Marisol ease off. "I like how they look there," Kim said. "They feel right." Kim now looked at art in a new way, she'd told Jane, since she'd met Waylon.

"That's it," Jane said. "They feel right." Jesse's shoulder touched hers.

"If you're sure," Jane's dad said, coming over and

opening the closet that held her toolbox, "I can hang them now."

Jane was sure.

"Kim's right," Marisol said. "It's the perfect space for them."

Then Kim and Marisol went to refill their wine and talk about family treasures while Mom helped Dad hang the small portraits. Jane asked Jesse if he wanted another of the craft beers Danny had tucked into the fridge last night, and they went into the kitchen.

The hanging of the portraits took all of five minutes, during which everyone filled their drinks and found a seat for the serenade. Once everyone was seated, Dad said, "Your mother's already heard this, but I wanted to try this out on you kids before I take it live."

George seemed pleased to be included in the "kids" category. Barb looked sleepy. Marisol muted the Lions game. They were losing anyway. Kim topped her wine glass, then Jane's, with the last of Jesse's delicious wine.

Dad explained that he had worked up a medley of Foreigner, a band Jane had been very fond of when in middle school and loved hearing again. When Dad sang, Barb chimed in with a soaring soprano, her gospel voice a revelation.

After the mini-concert was over, and everyone clapped, softly so as not to wake Susan, Jane's dad asked Barb if she'd like a side gig. For the first time, Barb acknowledged she was pregnant by patting her still flat tummy. "I think I'll be busy doing other things," she said. George burst with pride and love. Jane thought it a beautiful sight.

Jane's friends stayed after her family had all departed, Mom carrying a large shopping bag of leftovers. Jesse and Jane sat on one of the sunroom loveseats. George and Barb sat on the other while Kim took the chair Jesse swung over from the living room for her.

"Would your daughter freak out if she knew you were dating Jesse?" Kim asked. "Happy to have her think Jesse's with me." Kim smiled, all mischievous innocence, and Jane was glad she'd rebounded so well from all the turmoil in her life.

"Jesse's as much a friend to me as you are, and I don't care who knows it."

"Oh, I think you're a little more than friends," Kim said.

Jane blew her a kiss.

"But you don't want to hurt Marisol," Barb said, and Jane agreed that much was true.

Jane thought she probably hadn't fooled anybody. Her parents had known her marriage had been loveless for many years; her kids had felt the distance between her and Stan. She hadn't told anyone except her therapist and her mom that she'd been laying the groundwork to divorce Stan. Having a professional therapist for a mother could be handy, but also a pain.

"I suppose your mom had you talk about your feelings around the murder?" Jesse asked.

"You suppose correct. The only reason they didn't cut their cruise short is because I told them I'm dating a homicide detective and an FBI agent lives next door."

"Former agent."

"Yes, and congratulations, you two!"

"You better watch out, Jane," Kim said. "Seems

like pregnancy is going around in this place."

"Ha ha."

Around the dinner table, George had told everyone, including Jane's family, the story of his past. They all took it in stride. Even Marisol.

"Barb went back to Detroit to resign, but her bosses asked her to stay on through the criminal trials, despite me being her former CI and her current love. She flew back to St. Pete to help me convalesce from the gunshot wound. You heard about the shoot-out at the Boat House, I'm sure," he'd said. At the time, Marisol seemed happy that Susan was too young to understand most words.

Jane was glad she'd managed to tell her kids about the entire two-day double trouble episode.

"So Barb was considering her options," George told the family with some delicacy, "but when she realized she was pregnant, I insisted she turn in her badge for good. We flew back to Detroit together to take care of final FBI business and marry at the courthouse with our families present."

Privately, Barb had told Jane days ago about George's romantic proposal in the food court of the Tyrone Mall after she'd shown him a ring she really liked. She had not shared that with the table, but now she filled in the story for Jesse and Kim.

"He sat me down with a soda and then said he'd be right back. He came rushing up five minutes later with a bag of fries. The ring I'd chosen was stuck on a french fry in the front of the bag." Barb held out her hand, showing the ruby circled with tiny diamonds.

"I had it worked out with the sales clerk," George said. "I told him. We come in, I give you the high sign, which was a thumbs-up behind Barb's back, she chooses her ring, and I'll be back in five minutes to pay for it. Cash. The fries were a last-minute inspiration since they were right there in the food court. She's always hungry now."

"Damn right," Barb said, smiling.

"Where'd you get cash, George?" Kim asked. She wasn't being rude. Jane had discovered retired people in St. Pete talked openly about finances. Everyone pooled their knowledge of ways to acquire extra money to pad out their pensions and social security. It was a kind, and sometimes necessary, courtesy.

"My brother paid me for a little job I did for him while I was in Detroit."

Jane raised her eyebrows at Barb.

"He helped his brother put a bar and a bathroom in the basement. They did it in three days!"

"What about your stitches?" Jesse said.

"I did the finish woodworking; it's a skill I've always had." George put his hand in the air and wiggled it back and forth in the universal symbol for not a big deal. "My brothers and dad did the heavy lifting."

"So there are more of you!" Kim said, laughing.

Jane cracked up just thinking about three more Georges. She laid her head on Jesse's shoulder. He put his arm around her and pulled her an inch closer.

"So you told your mom you were dating Jesse?" George asked.

"Yes. And she told my dad. They're fine with it. I haven't told my kids yet because it's early days."

Jesse placed his hand on Jane's. Kim saw the gesture. "Anyway, you never know," she said, "he may dump you tomorrow."

Everyone laughed. Jane got up to hug Kim and walk her to the door. Barb and George followed them out. Nobody had to drive. Barb and George had signed a long-term lease and were staying put next door. Kim would never dream of moving away from her bayou. Jane was more content than she could ever remember feeling. Waves of happiness rippled through her heart right to the skin tingling on her body.

Jesse had come with Jane to see the neighbors out the door and make sure Jane locked up. They walked down the hallway, and Jane tugged Jesse toward the bedrooms for the first time. She had done a lovely refresh of the bedclothes since he'd last seen them. She'd even bought new pillows. She pulled down the duvet on one side and then the other and Jesse came up behind her and unzipped her peach-colored dress. Jane thought nothing was as sexy as a zipper. Well, except the buttons on Jesse's shirt.

"I bought you a toothbrush," Jane said.

"Guess you love me," Jesse said.

"Guess I do." Her mouth found his in the dark. "Love you."

All we really need is each other, Jane thought, as she drifted to sleep in her lover's arms. Everybody else in the world they loved was just frosting on the cake.

A word about the author...

JANE IN ST PETE is Cynthia Harrison's seventh novel with The Wild Rose Press. She lives in Detroit and St. Petersburg with her husband. They have two grown sons and three grandchildren.

Since 2002, Cindy has been blogging at: www.cynthiaharrison.com

Thank you for purchasing
this publication of The Wild Rose Press, Inc.

For questions or more information
contact us at
info@thewildrosepress.com.

The Wild Rose Press, Inc.
www.thewildrosepress.com